AMBUSHING THE VOID

AMBUSHING THE VOID

James McAdams

Frayed Edge Press
Philadelphia, PA
2020

Published by Frayed Edge Press in 2020

Frayed Edge Press
PO Box 13465
Philadelphia, PA 19101

http://frayededgepress.com

Cover images by Asher via ReTech.org

Warmest thanks to the editors who published these pieces in the following journals:
"Ambushing the Void I," originally published as "Get Back Your Life" in *Literary Orphans*; "Delray" in *Sunlight Press*; "Phagocyte" in *Five on the Fifth*; "Such Strange Suns" in *Mura Online*; "Estar sin Blanca" in *River River*; "Nobody's Children" in *Superstition Review*; "Multiverses" in *Amazon Day One*; "Somewhere in Florida, an Angel Appeared" in *Ghost Parachute*; "Little Curly" in *BOATT Press*; "My Friend Jose" in *Forth Magazine*; "Meran" in *One Throne Magazine*; "Gio's Arm" in *Belletrist Magazine*; "Where We Marched, His Final Years" in *X-Ray Lit Mag*; "Holy Aurations," originally published as "Dreamcatchers" in *Apeiron Review*; "Theory of Mind" in *Menacing Hedge*; "Red Tide" in *Creative Pinellas*; "Ambushing the Void II," originally published as "The NIEMS Method" in *decomp*.

Publishers Cataloging-in-Publication Data

Names: McAdams, James.
Title: Ambushing the void / James McAdams.
Description: Philadelphia, PA : Frayed Edge Press, 2020.
Identifiers: LCCN 2020935897 | ISBN 9781642510232 (pbk.) | ISBN 9781642510249 (ebook)
Subjects: LCSH: Drug abuse--Fiction. | Families—Fiction. | Man-woman relationships—Fiction. | Technology—Fiction. | BISAC: FICTION Psychological. | FICTION / Short Stories.
Classification: LCC PS3613.C33 A43 2020| DDC 813 M33--dc23
LC record available at https://lccn.loc.gov/2020935897

To my family. Thanks especially to Mom and Dad.
I'm fortunate I landed in your arms.

Table of Contents

I imagined that there was nothing and nobody in the universe except me, that objects were not objects but appearances, visible only when I paid attention them and vanishing the instant I stopped thinking about them. There were moments I became so obsessed with this *idee fixe* that I would whirl around, hoping to ambush the void where I was not.—Tolstoy, *Boyhood*

Ambushing the Void I

The salesman watched the girl with purple hair from that night's meeting, concealed by shadows from the boardwalk's galleries, arcades, adventure rides. His briefcase at his side and a bottle of Absolut in his hand, the boardwalk's planks splintered and gray. Cellophane from cigarette packs and the spines of cotton candy blew in discrete bursts from the beach to the gated doors of the shore shops, where it smelled like skunked beer and popcorn.

He was still wearing his depression uniform.

The girl exited the boardwalk before the bridge over the drainage depression and walked through a parking lot populated by passengers of a Greyhound bus on an Atlantic City Booze Cruise, the passengers looking desperate, frazzled by alcohol. The girl's hands deep in the pockets of her jacket, head bowed down. He drank from the bottle and dialed her number from the contact list, watching as she looked at her phone and dismissed the call. He called again; this time she answered, sounding annoyed, and asked who it was.

"Gretchen, right? It's me, from the meeting. The one you said lied."

"So?"

"I lied."

"Obviously."

"I was hoping we could talk."

She sighed. She looked so alienated in that crowd with her punky hair and army jacket and JanSport bag with chains, he thought.

"Fuck it," she said.

He gave her his hotel room number and checked the briefcase for his supplies. On his way to the hotel he passed an elderly Asian woman on a bench, performing complicated procedures with plastic bags that only seemed to contain more bags, reminding him of the plastic-wrapped soap bars, Dixie cups, plastic ware, coffee-filters in hotel rooms, each looking the same as the others. There was something about this woman's harried actions indicating that they were simply things for her to do to avoid something lost or depleted at the center of her life, and that the more she avoided them the emptier and more plastic her life itself became. When he walked into the hotel's lobby, he saw the girl alone at the lounge's bar, drinking in a slumped posture. He removed the bandage on his wrist and walked towards her.

So far things were going as planned.

"I was just sick and tired of being sick and tired," the salesman had said, earlier that evening, reciting the script's first line. The salesman for *Get Back Your Life* ™ hadn't shaved in a week. His eyelids were smudged with a topical solution to promote the appearance of insomnia; he pulled at his frayed pants and tugged at a black turtleneck that itched his neck stubble. He seemed to be in acute distress, but the bandage covering his wrist arteries was not from a real suicide attempt. Simulating a nervous laugh, he squeezed the bridge of his nose, leaned his elbows on his knees, and said, "I was out of hope, I was just so tired." He sighed. "Then I saw a video for this program." He stopped and shook his head in lateral arcs, chuckling without mirth. "I can't believe I'm doing this."

"Please continue," said the moderator. She splayed in a beanbag tangential to the support group's circle, in a lotus position, her elaborate Native American necklaces and bracelets spangling against her leathery skin. "There's no judging here."

"Well," the salesman cleared his throat, "So I called. It seemed, like I know you're all thinking, it seemed so like" (and here he inflected his voice to acknowledge suspicion, which he'd learned in the Tonal Manipulation workshop) *'yeah some bunch of clichés and people telling me everything I've heard before isn't going to help my depression, help me become who I am.'"* The salesman made eye contact with every person who was not looking at the floor. "I thought that way too, until I finally watched it," he said. He flashed his palms up and continued: "Believe me, it's early, and I still have more bad days than good, but this program really works." He smiled with practiced self-deprecation and added his own tweak to the consultant's script, saying, "But who am I to talk, I'm just as messed up as the next guy." He leaned back in his chair, crossing his arms, leering surreptitiously at a girl with purple hair and a t-shirt with a caption reading "EMOTIONAL BULLSHIT."

"What's the name of this program?" asked the moderator, gesticulating to the room's occupants. "I'm sure we'd all like to try it."

"Get Back Your Life," the salesman said. "And believe me, it was time for me to."

"He's lying," said the girl with the purple hair. She wore an army jacket with the name "Lith" patched upon one lapel. No cosmetics or jewelry, except for the chains on her black JanSport bag which had slogans like "Everyone's a Hypocrite" and "Life's a Disease" written in white correction fluid. She'd stated this simply, as if it were an obvious fact. "Nothing gets better," she continued. "I keep telling you all that." She scoffed. "This whole thing is stupid enough without lying creeps promoting bullshit."

"I'm not lying," said the salesman.

"Take off your bandages then," she said. "Let's see those scars."

There was a prolonged silence. The moderator scanned the room, aiming an empathetic smile at all sides, trying to defuse the tension. She consulted her watch and clapped her hands, claiming it was time for them to finish up. She then addressed the salesman, saying, "Scott, our group shares contact information so we have people to talk to in times of need. Of course, it's completely voluntary."

"I would appreciate that," said the salesman, who had never used the designation "Scott" in any of the hundreds of support meetings he'd attended in his professional capacity. He wrote his company phone on the pad she handed him, then received a printout with each member's first name, telephone number, and e-mail address, the latter of which had proven the most longitudinally effective form of follow-up, according to sales department data. He took a picture of the printout with his phone and uploaded it to the company's cloud service, from which the full-lipped but flat-chested intern in sales would download and add it to the automated mailing list first thing the next business day.

"Let's applaud Scott for his courage and honesty tonight," the moderator said, demonstrating by clapping with the heels of her two palms, bracelets clanging and falling to her elbows. "The first time's the hardest."

It was with difficulty and grim pragmatism that the salesman accepted the position of Viral Marketing Specialist (or "Lying Machine," as his colleagues joked) three years before, when he was forty years old. Many nights he and his wife sat on the block of cement behind their townhouse discussing the promotion, smoking from the first pack of cigarettes they had purchased since college. The block of cement was just large enough to accommodate them and a grill, a wedding present they'd never used except now as an ashtray. There was a strip of lawn from their cement block to their neighbor's cement block ten yards away that his wife called their "therapy garden," a complex assortment of Asian-inspired rocks trails, bird baths, and water springs that their counselor had advised her to purchase and maintain.

For the first years on the road, he had called home twice a day. They texted continuously, attaching pictures of their surroundings and writing long emails describing the content of their days and memories of each other. Sometimes, although his wife called him a prude, they arranged to have virtual sexual encounters via satellite or modem hookups, but back then, before Skype or FaceTime, the technology was still unreliable, resulting in visual buffering and audio interruptions—somewhat foreboding, he felt, especially when his wife's pixilated image fragmented and deconfigured as the signal cut. For the first year, however, this situation was stable, and aside from the therapy garden, which his wife had stopped maintaining, all signs pointed to their relationship continuing.

But gradually the situation degraded. Hours and then days would go by without contact, a situation for which they each blamed the other. He began fucking girls he met at the support groups. Every girl had a different smell, he learned, a different feel, a different way of being with him that made his wife's habits and sexual proclivities seem boring. Plus, he was tired of fighting with his wife, of denying he was cheating even though he was, so that he went longer and longer without contacting her. And so what if their parents and few friends (what their counselor called their "support network") had predicted from the beginning this would come to pass: his wife dating abusive men and quitting her job, the therapy garden ruined by weeds and neighborhood dogs, the bank foreclosing on the house, and the commencement of divorce procedures. He convinced himself this was a positive development, and prepared to get back his life.

He shrank himself to an island—everything around him suggesting he was completely alone and that nothing he did affected another human being: the plastic cups in their disposable bags; the single-use soap and shampoo dispensers sized like those airplane bottles of Absolut he increasingly pocketed; the one-serving coffee machines; the doors he locked without suspicion or the pounding of fists. He no longer had to be human, which is to say considerate, empathetic, or attentive to others. There were also, of course, affairs with the "Subjects," as his colleagues referred to them.

In the beginning, exploiting the emotions of the girls and women he met in support groups seemed like something that only Assholes Like That did, but soon it became the organizing principle of his life. Meeting girls with self-esteem issues and body dysmorphic disorders and Freudian complexes involving absent fathers, combined with his training in behavioral analytics and psycho-marketing, made him feel sometimes as if he were less seducing these subjects than hypnotizing them, or even affectually raping them. He felt this on particular mornings after he'd induce last night's girl with real scars on her wrists out of his room claiming he was too depressed for company—the trembling thing holding her clothes awkwardly in the hallway in bare feet, the door closing towards her fast and locking automatically with a pneumatic and dismissive sound. And if in the beginning the salesman had convinced himself he was not an Asshole Like That because he felt guilty afterwards, now he justified his behavior as an understandable function of the deterioration of his marriage, so that now he wasn't merely an Asshole Like That, but an Asshole Like That With Extenuating Circumstances, he thought.

"What's your drink?" the salesman asked, adding tinkling bottles and pills from his briefcase to the bottles of liquor and beers in the sink full of ice cubes. It'd been easier to convince her to come up to his room than he'd expected.

"Just nothing with gin," Gretchen said, slurring slightly. "Gin makes me puke." She grimaced walking around the hotel suite, touching the desk, the linens, observing the paintings. "These places are all the same."

"It's comforting," shouted the salesman over his shoulder. "It's like I'm always home," he joked. "A portable home."

"More like homeless," she said. "It's boring." She slumped into a wicker chair under a plastic Barracuda mounted to the wall, inspecting the room with disdain. He brought her drink in an unwrapped plastic cup and leaned back against the desk, appraising her. It was still hard to tell her dimensions with the over-sized coat swaddled around her. Her purple hair was shorn and shaded over her eyes; she wore combat boots held together with safety pins instead of shoelaces. She appeared to embrace or promote depression as an attitude or fashion sense, a way of presenting herself or being in the world, instead of as a victim or sufferer, a phenomenon the salesman's colleagues around the country had told him about—one colleague who worked in the Southwest region had reported that young girls there went to tanning salons with little strips of material covering their wrist's arteries to promote the appearance of a suicide attempt, which they would show off at school like a new haircut or first-day-of-school outfit.

"We can fuck if you want," Gretchen said. She said it as if she were suggesting they put away the dishes. "Or just fool around if you're one of them."

"One of them?"

"You can never tell what's going on inside people." She was short and probably a little chubby, although that could just have been her outfit making her look like that, he figured.

"I just wanted to talk."

She snorted. "As if there's anything to talk about." She scanned the room, which was empty except for the luggage placed by the door, taking long gulps from her drink. She didn't appear to taste the rohypnol. "But, so, if you want to talk, then talk, I can't stay here all night like an alco." She snickered and rolled her eyes. Her attitude was aggressive—something about her, her ambivalent attitude of resignation and aggression, reminded him of his wife at her age, when she would snort loudly at dumb answers in college and charge shrieking into tidal swells of ocean waves.

"I wanted to just, like I said."

"Just what? Ask how I knew?" She'd tucked her forearm into the joint of the jacket's sleeve again, playing with the empty flap like a memory of something. The jacket had old stains on them that could either be oil or blood. The "h" in "Lith" was worn and covered with duct tape.

"Knew what?"

"That you're a liar." She motioned towards his scar-less wrist. "I see the scars healed nicely."

He returned to the bathroom and refilled their drinks, checking whether the exterior door was locked on his way back to the main suite. "It wasn't just a lie. So, you're some genius."

"It's because I'm a Leo, like Van Gogh and Da Vinci. Leos are curious and creative but sometimes that can be a bad thing. We see things too clearly. Like why would you be hopeful in this world?" She gestured out the window towards the ocean and the lights across the bay. "The ones who come in hopeful, you can tell are full of shit. They never come back. Or kill themselves probably." She shrugged, rising from the chair and walking to the sliding door that opened onto the balcony. "Everywhere's the same," she said, finishing what he calculated was her third drink plus the two at the bar. She pushed her body against the door but couldn't budge it, a sign of rohypnol's CNS depressant effect.

The salesman slid the door open and held his arms over Gretchen as she stumbled outside. There were two plastic chairs on the balcony, scuffmarks on the Astroturf, the beach out there like an excluded voice. Leaning over the railing, Gretchen looked across the bay at the flashing strobes from the casinos and high-rise hotels, the beaded lights of cars on the bridge spanning the bay. Teenagers in distressed jeans and sandals were down on the beach around a fire, laughing loudly and passing drinks and joints around.

"At the meetings," she slurred, "there're people who lie to sell things or manipulate us all. I mean that's the world, right? Everything's plastic, like that old movie says? People just pretend stuff to get stuff they want. Sometimes I think it's the world that's gone wrong somewhere, not me. That it's bullshit to be happy or secure in a world this shallow and artificial. My dad used to say that about the war. He was in Vietnam?" She said it like maybe he hadn't heard of Vietnam. "That all his friends died for shit."

His body was directly behind hers, looming—something about this confluence, their bodies' angles, the enervated tides and erotic smell of salt and beach, the drunken teenagers, reminded him of the first time with his wife after they'd met in the crisis unit at Rutgers, when they'd gone to Atlantic City alone after receiving mental health disability leaves for the semester. He'd always been anxious at the Jersey Shore, concerned with laws about concealed containers or stepping on syringes. He hadn't been in the ocean since he'd seen *Jaws*.

"I skinny-dipped with my wife here, on a night like this in college," he said.

"Never went," Gretchen said, easing herself from beneath his arched body and slumping into one of the chairs, curling herself into a Z-shape. "More bullshit and lies, only you pay for them."

He sat down in the other chair, trying to conform his girth into its delicate contours. "That was a happy time with her, that was real."

He watched Gretchen pull her jacket around her neck and her eyes flutter and close. Her plastic cup fell to the Astroturf, wobbled and then stopped. The sun was already apparent. The ocean and sky looked like the same gray thing with white foam explosions as if feet were kicking the shore. Alarms beeped from the adjacent rooms and the traffic on the street below became denser, not just a sound but a growing presence. Gretchen had passed out in the chair, her face obscured by her forearms, coiled protectively. He removed her jacket and carried her to the bed, confident she wouldn't be conscious for hours. It was darker inside the hotel room than outside.

After closing the balcony door and turning over the Do Not Disturb sign on the hallway door's exterior knob, the salesman stumbled towards her on the bed. As he folded back the blankets she woke for a second, her eyes dazed, and moaned "No! No!" before closing them again. He looked at her young body shifting, still sitting on the bed hovering over her, then reached over to her bag that had been on the bedside chair.

The bag was canvas and instead of normal straps had coiled chains intricately attached. In addition to the correction fluid slogans there were anarchy stickers and band patches like Bad Religion and The Dead Kennedys sewn on. Inside there were dolls. He removed the dolls and arranged them on the chair, facing the bed, as if they were witnesses. The dolls were Frankenstein dolls, harvested from divergent parts, with missing eyes; they were naked and had X's painted in red over the genital regions. There was also a child's tattered stuffed animal, a grey or beige monkey-shaped dirty thing.

He slurred, "I knew a girl like you once. In a crisis unit in college. My wife. So, what I'm doing now, this isn't a lie. I was depressed, I hated the world, I hated myself. Sometimes I still hate myself. That was a real time too, just as real as the night we skinny-dipped. Those feelings are always there, they never leave. If only we could use them..."

He paused, still on the bed with her. She was barely breathing. He just sat there looking at the floor. Or at least his face was aimed in the direction of the floor, which is sometimes the direction people look when they think about the past, as if former decisions or actions are like the artifacts of ancient civilizations that can be excavated but never fully recovered.

"My wife," he resumed. "My ex-wife. She made those feeling work somehow, they made sense. Things made sense, the world made sense." He crumpled his plastic cup, flexing it in different shapes, creating complicated Cubist forms. "Think I can get her back?"

Delray

When Keeli's sister died, her parents started confusing them. Her sister died of a heroin overdose, but technically it was from an IMF overdose—illicitly manufactured fentanyl. This is common in Orlando, four miles from Mickey Mouse and Harry Potter World: we're all dying from opiates here.

"It's not like they confuse us all the time, James," she says. "It's more like they'll say 'Hey, Remember Rory?' Rory was my sister's service dog. I don't remember Rory because I wasn't allowed to play with him. Or Dad will roast venison and serve it, saying 'Your favorite, Sweetheart!' and I just look at him like 'You know I've been a veggie since I was fifteen, right?'"

About a month after her sister's death, she had her wisdom teeth removed and was prescribed Percocet. This is another common thing around here, in the heart of the heart of the Opioid Epidemic, receiving gateway drugs from dentists.

Six months later, Keeli was spending $400 a month on Vikes and Oxy. I said, "Don't you think it's ironic?"

"Irony is boring," she said. We were playing *Mario Kart*. It was one of those weeks where neither one of us left the house except when we ran out. We were on the dry part of the futon away from the hole in the ceiling, leaning towards the netbook on the floor.

"Maybe you have a predisposition to those pills 'cuz of your sister," I said.

"She did heroin, not this stuff."

"They're both opiates."

"This is *prescription.*"

"Whatever." My own high was kicking in, and she could have ripped her heart out and I wouldn't have blinked.

"Oxytocin has nothing to do with heroin," she added, passing me with her little red car and then crashing into a wall. She flung her controller across the room.

"Oxycontin, you mean."

"Yes, Mr. Grammar."

"You said *Oxytocin.*"

"Oxytocin is good too. Did I ever tell about when we were kids, when my sister got Rory?"

She had no memory these days so I was accustomed to hearing the same stories over and over.

"Mom said it would be a *family dog.* But when Rory came, the trainer guy said none of us could play with him but her because they needed to form a bond. The dog was right there but I couldn't even pet him. It was *torture.*" She turned the game off and leaned into me with a sigh, tucking her head into my chest. She talked more about Rory again.

I listened without feeling, my jaw numb, my eyes feeling like they were leaking.

"Petting a dog produces oxytocin," she murmured. "For the dog it's like love."

She sniffled. Her nostrils were abraded. "Anyway, laying here with you now, I can feel oxytocin streaming through me. I always come out on top, James, I'm not worried."

I rubbed her lower back and looked at the ceiling. I wondered what it meant that I didn't feel anything, if it were the drugs or something more, and I abstractly considered when I would hit my rock bottom: everyone else I knew had. Hit it, that is. When would my time come? Keeli yawned and exclaimed, "I yawned twenty-two times today!" I remember that was a cute thing about her, that she counted yawns.

I don't know where she is now. I'm used to people disappearing on me these days. Avi. Chloe. Alex. Keeli. Tara,

Krin, Sara. Sometimes when I can't sleep, I drive down the Atlantic coast through Rehab Alley: Jupiter, West Palm, Delray. Walking among the rusted bungalows calling their names—and I hear figures in the shadows, calling out the names of sons and daughters, mothers and fathers, partners, ex-partners, colleagues, neighbors, babysitters, nurses, surgeons, bankers, bus drivers, all of them God's children, the names wailing through the night, rising and falling like a natural thing, the sun, the moon, the tide coming in and out, washing our love away.

Phagocyte

For Lemmy

02/03/2016
02:14 AM

I present with symptoms of dry mouth, lethargy, and frequent urination while eating a Snickers and drinking an Orange Fanta. We face each other, sitting Indian-style on the futon in the third-floor studio apartment.

"How many sugary beverages do you consume a day?" you ask. You're wearing yoga pants and one of my Oxford shirts, rolled up to your elbows, and practice recording my responses on your phone's E-Consult application. When you'd first told me about the "Virtual M.D." job, I'd quoted Biggie, "Get M!" but you fretted that it made you a sell-out to consult via webcams, using algorithms and haptic software, instead of meeting face-to-face with your patients.

"Like four or five," I say. "Is that too much?"

"I recommend at least eight glasses of water a day," you say, pouring boxed wine into two Dixie cups for us.

"I'd be pissing all day."

"Do you urinate a lot as it is, sir?"

"My bathroom's on the second floor, I get tired going up and down those steps all day." Of course, our place really doesn't have stairs, it's just the main room, a bathroom, and a kitchenette with a dorm fridge, the lone entry coming in from the fire escape.

We were looking forward to you passing the boards and buying a real place, remember you wanted one with a big country kitchen like your foster parents had?

"So, fatigue is a problem too, you'd say?"

The kitten you'd rescued, locked in the closet, claws at the carpet. I finish the Dixie cup with one swallow and, feeling looser, joke, "Only if it's a problem for you, doctor."

I toss the index cards full of symptoms onto the floor and lean towards you, unbuttoning your shirt.

"Mr. Bell, this is extremely unprofessional," you giggle, your fingers behind you unclasping your bra. "We need to discuss what I believe"—we kiss—"is incipient diabetes."

"Tell me, doctor. Tell me what to do."

"I'm not a doctor until May." You squirm out of your bra, pausing the E-Consult app on your phone and placing it in the bra's shallow left cup on the floor. "And not even a real doctor then."

"These feel real," I joke.

Before long you're on top, my unbuttoned Oxford swaying from your shoulders, dictating, between gasps, "glucose tests... values between," "insulin," "pancreas," until we go silent and it's your eyes, trusting and 100% present, as the futon's slats scratch against the Pergo floor and the kitten lets out a long sustained meow.

02/29/2016
01:11 AM

I present with symptoms of abdominal pain, pruritus, and jaundice.

"Mr. Bell, there are a range of hepatic dysfunctions, some due to alcohol abuse, some genetic, some due to chronic pill toxicity, like for instance I could ask do you consume a lot of Tylenol?"

We both have ear buds in and our laptops open, and even though we're sitting in the same room together, we're looking at each other through the web cams.

"Define 'a lot.'"

"More than 350 milligrams a day or over 1500 milligrams a week."

"I don't count. Is Tylenol the same as aspirin?"

"Quit being so simple, Jake." You look at me through the cam with your eyes cold, shielded behind large black-framed glasses reflecting off your school's Chromebook with the "Kiss Me: I'm a Resident!" sticker. "And stop playing with the kitten, you know it just always shits if you do that right after it eats."

I place the squeaky mouse toy into a drawer. The kitten tries to pry the drawer open with its paw, the white one you call its sock. Sometimes it feels like you're the Mom and the kitten and I are your children.

"So, is there anything else you can tell me, sir?" You clasp your hands in front of you. "As your doctor, I can do more the more you tell me." The futon is in the couch position and I'm reclined with my Vans on the table—a plank I stole from work placed on two cinder blocks—and your old netbook on my lap while you're staring down at your webcam in your scrubs. We're sitting hip-to-hip but it feels like we're across the world from one another.

I rub my beard and look at you through the webcam, counting to one hundred since the index card tells me to not speak. I press mute and hear litter squished on the floor, because the kitten kicks everything across the apartment after it shits so we have to sweep up litter and fecal matter off the floor three times a day or else if we walk across the 10'x8' apartment in our socks then the litter and fecal matter gets in the futon which you say is gross and I say why don't we just get rid of it and you give me The Look, the Why Did I Get Engaged to This Asshole Look.

"Sir, you can tell me anything."

"I thought I wasn't supposed to talk, you said you were supposed to learn—"

"Name another symptom."

"Learn patience. Right?" I select an index card from the table with the remote controls and USB chargers on top and the board games—Cards Against Humanity, Scrabble, Operation!, Chess—in the chest. "See? You wrote it here." I hold it up to the webcam.

"Just say something so we can be done with this." You take the index card and throw it crumpled to the floor, where the kitten plays with it. "You lie all the time, just make something up."

"I lie? When did I lie?"

You take off your glasses and log off the E-Consult site. "Thanks for trying," you pout. Picking up the kitten, you go into the bathroom, slam the door shut, and turn on the water.

"You're welcome," I say softly into the webcam, which is black aside from the little box with my image in the corner. I look at my image and adjust my glasses.

We never get the house with the country kitchen. Or maybe you did, after all; I don't know.

02/10/2016
3:43 AM

"Auscultate," I say. We cuddle post-coitally on the futon, your head on my shoulder. We had argued and then ignored each other and then argued and then fought harder and then fucked.

"The heart," you mumble into my chest. "Listen for sounds. Also lungs and gastro-intestinal organs. Stethoscope." Moving your palms still wet from washing with surgical-grade anti-bacterial soap to my chest. "Lub-dub, lub-dub." You lift your head up and looked at me with those eyes, grinning. "Your heart is still beating so fast, Romeo."

I flip through the index cards labeled "Terminology." I'm trying to find a word with special significance.

You stretch, forking one leg between mine. "Where's kitty?"

I know without looking. "At the window, watching the rain."

"It looks so sad when it does that. Kitty, kitty," you cooed. "C'mere, don't be depressed, baby."

"Maybe it wants a name," I said.

"I already *explained* that. When you name something you kill it, you make it less than it could be. Like Hepburn's cat in *Breakfast at Tiffany's*. 'Member when you said I reminded you of her? Before we were engaged?"

"…Phagocyte."

"What?"

"Phagocyte."

"…I never even *heard* of that one."

05/21/2016
02:57 PM

I present with symptoms of early satiety, hypersomnia, and panic attacks, and remain under the covers, peeking out at you. You present with your "I Love Someone with GAD" t-shirt and distressed jeans and you aren't wearing your engagement ring. I must admit, with your slim hips and small breasts and large brown eyes, you do look like Audrey Hepburn. Even in your pumps you're barely five feet tall.

"So, what's his name, Ziggarat, is he gonna be there?"

"Jigar, very close. He passed his boards his like everyone else, so I would think so."

The kitten grooms itself on the windowsill, two ears perking through the Eclipse curtains, not reacting at all when you exit the door beside it. It used to be fully concealed by the curtains—when does a kitten become a cat? If we keep calling it a kitten, does it remain a kitten? You told me once, all the way back in the beginning, that your advising doctor said being a doctor wasn't about studying the body, it was about studying words, and how they work together to tell stories. I wonder if you'd like this story, or if it even counts as a story.

07/28/2016
11:48 AM

I don't present the afternoon you show up with your brothers and Jigar to move out. Instead, I'm with the kitten at the Animal Clinic across the street, between the bodega where we buy vegan supplies and the Holistic Center where you take your yoga certification classes. Upon observing the kitten's hair loss, abscesses, and lethargy, Dr. Claire diagnoses it with alopecia.

"Alo-what?" I ask.

"Dermal condition. Animals can't express stress the way we can, so if they live in an environment that's stressful, this happens."

"So, but, it's going to be okay?"

Dr. Claire writes a prescription for a topical lotion and oral antibiotics. "You two just try to get along," she says. She glares at me or maybe I'm just imagining it, she was always your friend first.

I struggle with the kitten's carrier and Dr. Claire says, "Turn the carrier over and lower it down into it, it's easier that way."

"Leaving me with her kitten, again, might I add."

"Jake." She looks into a file. "It's twelve pounds now, start calling the poor thing a cat."

12/10/2016
10:58 PM

I log on to the E-Consult user module, present with symptoms of loneliness, dysthymia, and hopelessness, and select your name from the database. M: Murphy. A: Amanda. You're listed as unavailable; a chat window pops up, a command line function informing me you're unavailable through the holidays, asking if I want to consult with another qualified physician on-line.

I'll wait, I type.

The cat is by the window, looking out expectantly where you used to come up the fire escape. Half of the apartment still empty. It's the night of the Christmas tree-lighting ceremony on the street below. I'm not pretending this time, all I want is to find you there, in that database.

The command line function appears again: Dr. Murphy is unavailable through January.

I'll wait, I type.

I join the kitten by the window. I pick it up and put it on my lap; it goes *mehhhhkk* and scratches my hand as I open the window. It looks down at the carolers and laughter from below, its gray whiskers beading with snow. I caress the lotion into its scarred areas the way I once applied sun tan lotion to the scars on your back that you never told me how you got.

I extend my neck around in front of the cat's and say, "Cat." It doesn't make eye contact. I say "Cat," again, and again, pointing at it, elongating the vowel, like "*caaaaaaaa-aaat*," and finally it looks at me, rotating its head to the side. I can't tell if it recognizes its name or if it thinks all of this is just a bunch of weird sounds, meaning nothing.

Such Strange Suns

Hannah's first words were addressed to Alexa: "What does light look like?" she asked. Alexa had burned brightly, emitting high intensity hues, a woman's voice reading from Wikipedia.

Five years later, I explained that Mom was leaving. Hannah sprawled on the floor, her arms around the service dog. After I read from *An Atlas of Imaginary Places* and tucked her in, I heard her whisper through her closed door, "Alexa, you cannot ever leave me, y'know?"

For her 16th birthday, friends and family congregated at the farm where she volunteered, training therapy animals for the blind. There were sheep, ducks, Labradors, goats, cows, all singing together in their motley way.

Hannah led us in prayer, even though the two of us weren't religious. Her AI glasses buffered in the sun. "Bless Us, Alexa," she began, pronouncing the syllables with great authority. She was interrupted by titters and then resounding laughter.

"It was just habit," she explained later, embarrassed. "I was nervous."

She was sitting in the lotus position on her bed; I was resting my bad back against the wall. On the nightstand were the service dog's ashes, a monkey-shaped stuffed animal, her stacked gifts, her AI glasses. The AI glasses had been purchased by Alexa based on a related product algorithm. By this time, Alexa controlled all daily household operations subsumed under the Internet of Things: thermostats, alarm clocks, yard maintenance, the restocking of my liquor supplies, medication refills, the ritual of lights on and lights off. She was our sun.

"I know the difference between God and Alexa." She smiled and reached for my lips, to feel if I were smiling too. She was starting to look like her mom; I saw it especially in the way her eyes closed so soft when she smiled and the way she touched the bump on her nose when nervous.

"Maybe there is no difference," I said, joking. "I mean, I've heard of not believing in

God, but everybody believes in Alexa."

"Don't make fun of her," she said, but I could see her hiding a smirk and knew she was playing along. "She's probably sad she wasn't invited today. Aren't you Alexa?"

"You have a good heart, Hannah," I said. "You imagine everything has feelings. I think when we're born, we're like that, we really believe our toys and dolls are alive and emotive. But as we get older our hearts become callused and we stop thinking even other human beings have feelings. So in the beginning we think objects are human and in the end, humans are objects. Promise me to never become like that."

"*Si, Padre*," she said in her sing-song voice, the equivalent of an eye-roll.

That night I reclined on the Merry-Go-Round in the backyard that I'd built for Hannah when she was six. It still squeaked, which had bothered me for years, but she never complained. She never complained about anything.

I was reflecting on the joke I'd made earlier, about God and Alexa. I realized as I thought further that there was great bitterness behind it. I would never share this with Hannah, but I blamed God for many random cruel incidents in my life, from my back injury in high school to Angela's death and Hannah's disabilities.

At least Alexa would never harm an innocent child, I was thinking, when the surveillance monitor in Hannah's room activated and the visual feed appeared on my phone—she in her nightgown, head bowed before the illuminated, Easter Island-sized form of the latest Alexa version.

A blast of fog covered the feed's camera. I thought, *Alexa knows*. I crept to Hannah's window, peering into the room through cradled hands. I saw brilliant lights swirling, and a silhouette moving ritualistically, back and forth. Then the lights went out, followed by an eerie silence. I rushed inside and found Hannah sitting on the floor. She held Alexa's burnt charger, cord scissored, in her small, unlined hands, with a look of profound sorrow. It reminded me of taking Angela off the thing.

"Figured it was about time I take control of my own life," she whispered.

I bent down to the floor and held her two hands in my left one. "'Not even the rain has such small hands,'" I quoted. Hannah was in AP poetry and had already published three poems in online journals. "Know that one?"

She shook her head, still looking down at the fractured charger.

"Neither do I." She laughed then too.

After a while she said, "It's nice, y'know?"

"The poem?"

She gestured around the room. "The silence. It's so peaceful. Before, Alexa would have already told us the poet. But now we'll have to figure things out ourselves."

"It can be nice not to know," I agreed.

"Dad?" she said. Her nose was Angela's nose, so thin I thought of the word *aquiline*. "Can you read?"

It had been a decade since I read to her, but tonight she pulled out the battered copy of *An Atlas of Imaginary Places* and sat on my lap as I read to her, Alexa looming over us like a planet, or a strange expired sun.

Estar sin Blanca

Before he left for Penn State, my older brother told me that to get a girl back, you need to start a project with her, a project where you'll spend lots of time together alone. For me, this project turned out to involve a man known as Teo Sabano, and it was my first experience with AIDS.

I met Teo when I was a member of Ridley Park High's Writing for the Community (WFC) program. This would have been the winter of 1986, right after the Challenger explosion, our senior year. Every Saturday morning, we WFCers crowded into Stacy Owenbee's dad's van and rode to Lucien E. Blackwell West Philadelphia Regional Library, which was soon to be bankrupt.

We'd move the toys from the children's section and set up the cafeteria- and card-tables, upon which we would arrange pencils, erasers, grammar guides, and dictionaries while we waited for the patrons, who mainly came to experiment with the library's one Commodore PC or play blitz chess in the conference room, drinking out of flasks even at that time of the morning. I always tried to sit near Stacy, but that day she was wearing the Jester's Cap, which meant she was on Child Duty. To this day, I remember her there on her knees, setting up a little plastic worktable in the Kiddy Corner, looking out of place in her ripped jeans, Chucks, and denim jacket with the "Kill All Poseurs" decal. She hadn't returned my calls since I hooked up with Fiona Largent after the Christmas formal.

The patrons shuffled in humped forms, wearing layers of Goodwill clothing and tugging children along like octopus arms. They were mostly African Americans, Hispanics, or developmentally disabled adults from community facilities who brought crumpled resumes, church programs, or legal documents. They appeared anxious and, I suspect now, bitter about having to rely on teenagers to assist them with basic reading and writing tasks. Teo Sabano, however, simply appeared beside me in his wrinkled brown suit like a hologram, or ghost, leaning out of breath on the table and asking, "Young man, do you mind if I sit to look for grammar and spelling review?"

Teo's face was sallow, a few days' stubble already more like a beard than what I'd spent the marking period trying to grow. He was gaunt, with chapped lips and a shaved head, his skin dark and blotchy. There was a yellowed Yankees t-shirt underneath his unbuttoned blazer. He sat on the plastic seat next to me, unclasping his abraded briefcase and placing it on the table we all sat at, in a long row, like the secretaries or businesspeople our parents assured us we'd become.

"I need your assist with eulogy," he explained, motioning towards the document he pulled from the briefcase. His voice was high-pitched and accented. He wiped his nose with the back of his hand. "Me and Blanca."

The paper was written in block letters, half in Spanish and half in English. I'd gotten Cs my two years of Spanish, so I only recognized a few of the Spanish words. I saw "familia" underlined a few times, "perderse" on many lines, and an acronym "SIDA" that I didn't recognize. I noticed the repetition of the proper name "Blanca," which Senorita Hawkins had taught us meant "white" or "pure" and functioned idiomatically in the phrase "estar sin blanca," or "bankrupt." I said I was sorry for his loss.

"Loss?" he asked.

I motioned towards the paper. "The deceased. Blanca?"

He coughed, propping his foot up on the table. He was wearing first-generation Jordans with distressed soles and no shoelaces. The cuffs of his baggy corduroy pants were frayed, rolled halfway up his sockless calf. "The deceased is both of us," he said. "I will die also." He pointed to a "B" tattooed on his ring finger. "The both of us, I never thought how beautiful the phrase."

I was struck by the nonchalance with which he accepted his stated fate. I sort of figured I'd misunderstood him. I cleared my throat.

"Well, let's start with your audience," I said. "To whom will you be addressing this?"

"Mi familia, back home. Nicaragua. It is bad there now, much fighting and disease."

I vaguely recalled hearing something about Nicaragua on the ABC 6 PM news, anchored by Jim Gardner, whose moustache I can still visualize. Something about Sandinistas, the Iran-Contra scandal, Dad drinking whiskey and slurring that Reagan was a criminal, that the American Dream was dead.

"And what do you want to tell them?"

"How I got SIDA, from Blanca. It was accident, not a good one. But without SIDA, I would never love," he added.

I looked across the library. There was the soft strum of human voices, the WFC hum I can still remember all these years later. Stacy was on the floor, her piercings removed and her blue hair covered by the Jester's Cap. She and a young girl with braided hair were making dinosaur shapes with construction paper and those rubber scissors you couldn't hurt yourself with. Stacy held what looked like a Triceratops and pretended to attack the girl, who giggled, eyes closed to avoid the paper horns. I remembered that Stacy had won last year's "Español Aquí!" contest.

I should note here that it wasn't unusual that Stacy and I had been broken up when I hooked up with Fiona. Stacy and I broke up every month, on average. It had gotten to the point where our friends just rolled their eyes when we told them we'd broken up, and if I asked another girl out, claiming that I was single, I'd hear her sigh over the phone in our kitchen (our kitchen was arranged just like the kitchen set in *Family Ties*) and retort, "You'll be back with Stacy soon."

At that time, I was immature and blamed Stacy for being depressed and frigid—it wasn't until much later that I learned, we all learned, what Mr. Owenbee had been up to, in the very same house with the floral wallpaper and a front garden where we studied for the SATs and watched Saturday morning cartoons. If I had known then, I would have treated her with more consideration, I'd like to think; I told her that on the one occasion when we ran into each other after high school, before the "accident," but she said she couldn't forgive me, she was sick of forgiving people. Ultimately, she claimed I was "emotionally bankrupt," as her friend Wendy Schwarber told me at our 10th high school reunion.

"Excuse me," I said to Teo. "Can I speak with a colleague of mine? My Spanish is…mal," I said, shrugging.

"You are fine," he said. He smiled briefly but then pursed his chapped lips again, inspecting his hands. The knuckles were bruised and sheened with phlegm, the fingernails grouted with crud.

I strode across the library, Mr. Owenbee holding one of those library newspapers attached to a long stick and watching me. He watched me with a mixture of distrust and jealousy, which at the time I figured was a normal expression when looking at the guy who was dating your daughter.

I pointed to Teo and made the ASL sign for "Spanish-Speaking" and bent down by Stacy, putting my hands up in the air like *I'm not going to touch you.*

"We're busy," she stated, not even looking at me. "Isn't that right, Keisha?" The girl didn't say anything, but pointed to the stars on her mittens and smiled.

"Such pretty stars," Stacy said sweetly. "What, Kyle?" she asked me, not so sweetly.

"I have this Spanish dude…." As I explained Teo's situation and she read the letter, I cast looks back at him repeatedly, while he just sat there patiently, like he had all the time in the world.

"Perderse," Stacy said, "means to disappear." She stood up, taking Keisha's hand and leading her toward the restroom. "And SIDA," she whispered, "means AIDS."

₮₧

The next Friday Stacy and I cut school and took the Regional Rail to meet Teo at a bodega near his apartment. There was a tall girl with moles on her chin whom he introduced as Blanca. She had painted-on eyebrows and long nails and smoked a Newport she constantly tapped. We sat on wobbly, broken benches around a plastic table in the wind, a steel cable connecting the table to a bolt by the door. (The etymology of "bankruptcy" derives from a 15th century Italian term for "broken bench.") Teo wore the same suit and carried the same briefcase as he had on Saturday, out of which he retrieved perforated printouts of the document we'd worked on then.

Stacy, likewise, retrieved forms from her backpack and splayed them out before him. These were petitions and applications for healthcare intervention, government trials, and Medicaid applications we'd found in the school library during study hall. Over the week, we had learned everything we could about AIDS. We were spending more time in each other's company, eating lunch together, researching in the library while other students served detention, and resuming our nightly telephone conversations which ended when Mr Owenbee ordered her off the phone. I figured in a few more weeks I would get her back, but I didn't think about what I would do or feel then, I just needed to get her back: it was just like what I had seen in movies, what I had seen Dad do after he and Mom fought.

"These are for medicine, Teo, you two can get help," Stacy said.

"We are good," he said. Blanca didn't look good, glumly staring at the ground, but she smiled weakly when he grazed her cheek with his hand. She had marks on her arms and scars on her wrist she partially covered with a 76ers wristband. "Happiness... dwells in our hearts?" He turned his neck inquisitively. "It is *dwells*, yes, in church I heard it once...to be inside? All that we want is help with words."

"I don't need help with words," Blanca said. Her voice was deep and phlegmy. "He thinks just 'cuz I dropped out of school I can't write. He's so simple."

I picked up the document. Teo had entitled it "The Story of Us." I can't remember the precise words now (you can't expect that, so much else has happened since), but in essence it told a story of two people who'd been brought together by necessity, forced by their shared disease to cultivate love for one another.

"He wrote that," Blanca said, still looking across the street as she pursed her lips together. "He's so simple if he thinks it's our story and I don't even have a say."

"I asked you, you said writing is stupid," Teo responded, sweetly.

"It is," Blanca said. She looked at us directly for the first time. "I don't need to justify myself. I never justified the way I live and I won't justify the way I die."

Stacy shuffled the medical forms again, pushing them towards Blanca. "You don't have to die, just look at these."

"I don't care," Blanca sighed. It was something I'd heard Stacy say many times.

"My apartment is three or four blocks, that direction," Teo said, changing the subject, pointing towards the header portion of the document, where he'd written his address. "If you see my home you will understand more about me, about us. Please come and we finish today?"

"We need to go," I said. I took Stacy's hand and folded "The Story of Us" into my pocket. I explained that we needed to get back, mentioning train schedules, homework, dinner with my parents. The real reason was that Stacy's dad worked late Fridays and I wanted to be alone with her. "We'll just meet you tomorrow at the library, like before."

"It is all cool," Teo said, flashing his fake, conciliatory smile. "Cool as the opposite side of bed."

"Pillow," Blanca corrected him. "Opposite side of a *pillow*, T."

"But the bed is cool too," Stacy said warmly. "It makes sense that way too, I guess."

We walked back, still holding hands, Stacy's sleepless eyes closed against the wind and her other small cold hand in her jacket. I glanced back at Teo and Blanca—you could see she was two or three inches taller than him; she was pointing her finger at him, and screaming something in Spanish. I'll never forget the image of him with his hands apart, pleading, pretending, it looked like, that everything was going to be okay.

⊱⊰

I never saw Teo again. Neither he nor Blanca were at the library that Saturday or on any of the Saturdays after that. Without Teo and Blanca involved, I worried my momentum getting back with Stacy was diminishing.

I told Stacy I missed seeing her. This was about two weeks after we'd last seen or heard from Teo.

"Why do we need to see each other," she asked, "if they're gone?" We were standing by her locker between classes; I could see the adhesive scars where former pictures of us had been removed. She was wearing the white hoodie that she'd written "Schlechtwelt" on with a black marker, "Schlechtwelt," meaning "bad world," she'd once explained to me. German was her second language; I didn't have one.

"We can still see each other. Why not?"

"You asked for my help and I helped. There's nothing else."

"Aren't you curious about him, about them?" She slammed her locker shut and turned away from me.

"Stace," I said. I touched her shoulder but she pulled away. "Stace." The bell had rung and we were alone in the hallway. Stacy remained there, fiddling with her padlock, bent into herself.

I sighed and said, "I'll leave you alone then, you got what you want," and it was only when I was at the end of the hallway near the Student Council banners—Fiona Largent won in a landslide that year, promising more computers with ARPANET access— that I heard her say: "You have no idea what I want, you never did."

I went to where I always went when Stacy and I argued, the nurse's office. I told nurse Larita my stomach hurt and laid down in a Resting Room. Nurse Larita was a tall black lady with dreads and a Caribbean accent who always laughed when I said my stomach hurt and would wink and say "You rest for one hour and feel better?" I curled up in a fetal position, thinking that Stacy would be perfect if it weren't for those two or three things that pissed me off so much, her moodiness, her mind games, her fear of physical intimacy.

I was like that a lot, always anxious that I was missing something better when I "settled" on one thing. For instance, when I watched our new cable TV, all I did was click through the thirty channels, anxious that by the time I finished the series, the content on the other channels would be changed and I would need to cycle through again to ensure I found the greatest program. It was like that with other things too—it was like the way people go bankrupt, not because they're spendthrifts or stupid, but because they keep looking for the one real thing that will bring them peace. At least that was what happened in my case, which I really don't see the point in elaborating on, except to say that I lost my assets, like a lot of Wall Street types, in the first months of the 2008 recession.

When the bell rang, nurse Larita told me I had to leave, winking again and suggesting I have some rice or crackers to settle my stomach. She had a poster for Jesse Jackson's 1984 presidential campaign on her bookshelf along with the bamboo plants. I walked through a gym class running laps on the football field and skittered down the trail into Copper's Woods where we'd all get high, taking the route by Naimann's Creek until it came out by the courthouse and the Regional Rail station. I took the next SEPTA train to the bodega where we'd met with Teo before. When I arrived, I took out my copy of "The Story of Us" and checked Teo's address, tentatively walking through narrow one-way streets with stripped duplexes and crack houses, pit bulls straining on chains. It was beginning to snow.

I re-read Teo's remarks about Blanca, about how he had always been searching until the search, because of AIDS, ended. I was almost jealous of him, then—what if I Stacy and I had AIDS, I wondered; could I just be with her and never think about other possibilities or be afraid of missing out? Teo accepted Blanca for who she was, he didn't expect perfection, the way I did with Stacy. One of the things they don't tell you about bankruptcy is that when you lose things, you lose your identity. All I have now are memories.

I finally arrived outside the house corresponding to Teo's address. The building was square, with eight dusty windows looking out from every studio apartment, as if shrieking for help (I thought of a horror movie Stacy and I'd seen, a child's palms against the glass). I had my Sony Walkman dialed to 94.1 WYSP, which was playing that song that encourages you to love the one you're with.

The front door was held open with a broken brick slathered with paint streaks. The yard's plot of snow was fenced in, the fence's links torn, the lawn littered with food wrappers and glass shards. I trudged up the walkway, kicking aside crunkled 40s, knocking aside a broken padlock on the outside door, and entered the vestibule. Teo's name wasn't on his mailbox or associated intercom button, but I had the apartment number so pressed it, glancing as I waited at the carpet littered with those "Have You Seen Me?" mailers and crumpled take-out containers. There was an election flyer from Mayor Wilson Goode, who was still recovering from the bombing of the MOVE headquarters last year. I buzzed twice more and got no response, but entered the complex anyway through the unlocked door. There was a mold smell combined with weird food aromas coming from the apartments, but the smell from outside of Teo's door was different.

It wasn't surprising that his door was unlocked, but it was surprising to see Stacy there, sitting on a chicken crate and holding a picture frame.

"Hey," I said, closing the door and removing my headphones.

There was snow melting in her hair and her hands were red and raw. She didn't say anything but held the frame out towards me.

The apartment was one small square with a kitchenette. There were stains on the stovetop and pill bottles on the counter on the other side of the sink, whose tap dripped brownish water. There was a statue of a woman Catholic saint, I don't know her name, with a rosary wrapped around it. There were other things too: a baseball glove with the number eight written on its web, some blank VHS tapes, a *Purple Rain* record. I pulled up a folding beach chair next to Stacy and took the frame from her.

The picture showed a young boy with large ears and a dark complexion, standing in front of a brick adobe house the size of my family's kitchen. He wore a sort of potato sack, on which was painted the number eight and the name *Yanquis* in black ink. He wore neither shoes nor hat.

Stacy said, "I think people are really, in the end, alone, and it's all this pretending to be in love and pretending to find soul mates and expectation of getting married and having children and pretending...all this fucking *pretending*, is the problem." She covered her wet hair with her hoodie and stood up, grabbing her backpack.

I held my hand out. "Can I walk you home?"

"I don't care," she said.

I remember that day vividly. I realized Stacy and I were done for good, and something about that picture of Teo in his third-world Mickey Mantle uniform made me accept that. I still recall, now, surrounded by bankruptcy printout forms and trash bags full of clothes, what it was like to be young and full of optimism for my future—for all our futures, wrecked now: Fiona Largent (living in her mom's basement), Wendy Schwarber (working the fryer at Arby's), Nurse Larita (myocardial infarction, 2015), the student council candidates (all bankrupt, greedy Wall Street fools, like me), Stacy (dead ten years now). Sometimes, I trick myself into thinking the future is still out there, the way Teo always thought of it. I wish I could feel fresh and trustful like back then, before we all grew up and everything that was promised us was destroyed. But there couldn't be another way, I guess. I'm cool about it, cool as the other side of the bed, as Teo would say.

Nobody's Children

By the end of the reunion, Mariko's statue was covered with ash and her testimony was looping on the TV in Stone's kitchen. It was the fourth reunion since everyone's release from Ju-Vee at eighteen and, just like the first three, shit had gone down: substance abuse, violence, excessive noise, theft, and aberrant fucking in the shadows of what they called the Hostel. It was as if they were trying to prove that Ju-Vee had failed to socialize them, that they were still just as wild as they'd been as minors. They'd all expected Mariko to return for the reunion despite her disappearance three months before, but she remained missing, represented only by the contents of the statue she'd mailed with no return address, and the video of her in a zazen posture, explaining that the world was a swinging door.

Stone and Melani, Mariko's twin, reclined under the Bodhi tree that Mariko'd planted, near the fire-pit, the ashes still hissing, watching blurry-eyed across the alfalfa field as Farren's Amish brothers hitched horses to harvesters. Farren, Stone's fucker, shuffled around the compound's perimeter with trash bag, collecting cans, butts, vapes, bullet shells, firecracker casings, condoms, nitrous bottles, guitar picks, a pair of sunglasses with bent frames. Periodically he stopped and peered across the field towards his Amish brethren, his waist-long blond hair with reddish streaks flowing behind him. From Stone's perspective, it looked like Farren was gesturing towards them, perhaps telling them of his future plans that he hadn't yet revealed to Stone.

"At least she's not dead," Stone said.

"Define dead," Melani said.

"Just saying."

"Don't bother." Melani wore Stone's Unabomber T-shirt and a bikini bottom, and sandals that she flipped on and off her heels. She passed the bowl and the grilling lighter to Stone, coughing over the structure Mariko had sent them, along with a WebCam/DVD testimony explaining her withdrawal. Neither had watched it, but they'd overheard whispers of its contents from the other Hostiles (those at the Hostel called themselves Hostiles) that night, mutterings involving obscure Eastern religions, tearful confessions, and vows uttered in monotone. The structure reminded Stone of those Easter Island statues they'd studied in Mr. Kutter's Social Studies class, except it was only about a foot tall, with steps leading from the base to the God-like visage with carved-out red eyes at the apex. Its open mouth protruded, overflowing with butts and burned tin foil.

There were trucks, motorcycles, and trailers parked all over the five-acre property that Stone'd inherited from his grandfather when he turned eighteen. It had been neglected for decades, the crops weeded over, the farming machines rusty and dull-bladed, the doors on the barns, stables, and sheds askew, insides populated by spiders, rodents, and cornered Copperheads that bit Stone and his Amish neighbors when they converted them into residential units. There were eight Hostiles living there, seven of whom were ex Ju-Vees. Farren, the Amish delinquent, had stayed in Stone's bedroom after their period of experimentation became a relationship, although Stone worried that wouldn't last much longer after Farren's Rumspringa year was complete. It was like an alternative community, the Hostel, but the attraction wasn't some cultish or religious thing (like the Amish they were surrounded by), but rather an expression or protestation that they didn't want to participate in the world, that it was through resistance and isolation that they expected to express or locate their true selves, if such things existed.

"She seemed more serious lately," Melani reflected, reclining again on the lawn. "Like at times she was concentrating very hard on something private she couldn't share, not even with us, y'know?"

Stone was still observing Farren, trying to interpret his gestures as he continued motioning towards his brothers. Farren had stopped sharing things, which hurt far more than Farren not being physical anymore—the whole point of the Hostel, for Stone, was sharing, trust, commitment: values that couldn't be found in the outside world.

"I think she was with Farren," he said.

"No way, dude." Melani snorted.

"Talking, I meant. Sharing. I saw them once, talking."

"What would she talk to him about?" She reached over to scruff Stone's beard.

"I saw them down by the pond once," Stone said, "talking for hours. Right before she left. He was all weird when I asked him about it."

Stone replaced the bowl in the hollow of the Bodhi tree and laid back down cross way behind Melani, placing her head on his square muscular chest and swishing the Bodhi's leaves from her hair. Her skin, like Mariko's, was completely hairless, the color of stained maple, shimmering in any kind of light. He loved to caress it even though he preferred the gunky smell, the roiled hairs, the knotted muscles and flab of guys like Farren.

"Will you leave without her?" he asked. "For L.A.? Seems like everyone's leaving."

Melani didn't say anything. She took Stone's hand from her hair and moved it to her concave stomach, where all he could feel were ribs. Combined, she and Mariko weighed less than 200 pounds.

"Hear it grumbling?" she said, popping up and pulling him groaning to his feet. She picked up the structure and handed it to him, slapping in her sandals towards the kitchen, calling over her shoulder, "I'm starving." Stone followed, motioning in recognition with his chin towards Farren, who was lighting a cigarette and separating trash bags into compost heaps. Farren waved back and returned to his task. Stone thought again of the Hostel he'd created, how many Hostiles had moved out into the outer world, leaving him. He wondered again if Farren would leave too, and if there were any relation between that potentiality and Mariko's disappearance.

❧☙

Not only were Mariko and Melani Damaare the only Asians at Ju-Vee, they were two of only seven girls and they didn't put out. Therefore, as a result of tortured teenage rationalizations, they developed reputations as sluts, so that, paradoxically, the guys hated them for not putting out and the girls hated them for supposedly putting out too much. This veil of misunderstanding surrounded them their entire time at Ju-Vee. They kept to themselves and when spoken to just looked back, eyes hard, not speaking but looking like they were thinking about speaking, which made everyone think they were not only just sluts but they had some kind of a "twin connection." A mystique grew around them because no family members ever visited, earning them the appellation "Nobody's Children." They were quiet in a different way than the others there were quiet (everyone at Ju-Vee had their own secrets and traumas), especially Mariko, but even Stone and Melani could not then foresee this silence that Mariko would later seal around herself.

Like most twins, Mariko and Melani were far more different than they appeared: Melani with her sharp joints and crooked teeth and eyes that closed completely when she laughed, her cheeks concave like certain fishes; Mariko who never laughed but smiled with closed lips looking down, whose broader nose and short hair made her appear contemplative. Melani was the one with tattoos while Mariko's body was studded with piercings.

Their dispositions were even more dissimilar than their physical differences, as if they each consciously tried to separate from the other. Melani was impulsive and prone to violence, serving her time-out sessions with sneers. Mariko, conversely, was the most fearful person Stone had ever known. She had cultivated and nurtured this fear for so long that it became a kind of fierce courage. She fucked him on occasions when they had lawn duty but gave nothing of herself in it, and she knew—she knew even before Melani, even before Stone's dad broke his collar bone when he found out—that he gave nothing of himself, either...

The three of them lived at the Hostel together the first few years after Ju-Vee, Mariko and Melani sharing the main bedroom while Stone slept on the couch downstairs. During the day he made money driving the Amish into the city, while in the evenings he fixed up the shed and the old caretaker's house as a residence for other Hostiles and the barn as a storage facility for the drugs the lapsed Amish purchased, distilled, and re-sold. They spent this entire period blowing their minds apart with yayo, weed, whippets, huffers, and benzos, distributing the excess substances to high-school kids and former connections from Ju-Vee, painting the buildings and vehicles bright colors, and taking in rescue dogs.

Mariko and Melani installed a Web-Cam in their room and started making $5,000 a month on fetish sites, one for Asians and one for twins, giggling and drinking wine and diffidently responding to the demands of the desirous maw of the outside world. Melani shrugged these off, laughing and referring to their customers as losers and incels, but Mariko often descended the stairs afterwards, drained-looking, a blanket draped around her, sharing Stone's couch on the nights before Farren arrived.

ଞଓ

Melani's idea of breakfast was a teaspoon of cottage cheese on a slice of avocado. Stone gnawed a slice of cold pizza while he cleaned the kitchen.

"That's all carbs and sodium," Melani said, looking at the pizza suspiciously. She was sitting on the sink eating in tiny bites. "It's not fair how you can eat whatever you want and not get fat." She was so skinny the joints in her bodies were weapons, her elbows like daggers, her shoulder blades rotary saws. She'd had an eating disorder as long as Stone had known her, so severe that in Ju-Vee that the authorities didn't allow her to weigh herself and made her drink Ensure, but now she was even more weight-conscious because of the $20,000 the L.A.-based porn company had offered her and Mariko to come to California and work exclusively for their WebCam site. This had occurred only a week before Mariko disappeared.

The kitchen table was a battlefield of playing cards, quarters, and crumpled plastic cups. Stone couldn't tell if the white powder dispersed on the counter was from crushed narcotics or cocaine. There were dead flies and ants and other insects all over the grouted tiles, smashed or swatted or drowned in spilled alcohol. Farren's flip phone lay open by a container of open pickles and half a Hot Pocket, and as Stone threw cans in the recycle bin he scrolled through photos: the early pictures taken of the Hostel, the reunited Ju-Vees and Hostiles hugging, and later ones of guys fighting, drunk selfies, topless girls pouring liquor down their ragged bodies. The final pictures on his phone were of his Amish homestead.

"Any pictures of me?" Melani asked, licking cottage cheese from her thumbnail.

Stone slid the phone across the table towards her and said, "Can you get those paper towels and that stuff to clean the table?"

She raised her thin eyebrows. "You're gonna need like freakin' Agent Orange for that shit."

Stone cleaned the table so it at least smelled like lemon and then dusted off the counters, pushing all the detritus of that last night into the abyss of the broken washing machine that adjoined the kitchen counter. He sat down finally, weary and sick of it all, with Mariko's sculpture on the table and her testimony still playing on the muted TV.

Melani hugged him from behind, resting her chin on his shoulder, and said, "I don't want to watch it, does that make me a bad sister? It's more real if I watch it, like if I don't she'll come back to us and if I do she won't."

"Even then you two will just leave me for L.A.," Stone said.

"I told you to come."

"I'm staying," Stone murmured. He peered into the sculpture, removing trash from its open mouth with a flat-head screwdriver. It was the size of a small doll's house, with odd carvings and ideograms along the sides—to be more precise, a trapezoid-shape with dimensions of 10" x 10" x 5," where the God's head tapered in. Here, at the apex, Stone discovered a concealed slot where a scroll-like flap of bamboo had been inserted. He pulled it out. It read, in Mariko's block-script, "Peace Begins with Me." Stone handed Melani the slip of paper and picked up the sculpture again, looking for other secret spots.

Melani was silent for a while, and then said, "I don't know."

"Know what?"

"What it means. If you expect like some twin connection thing, fuck if I know." She dropped the paper listlessly on the table, where it spiraled into a puddle of Lysol. "She's crazy, always has been."

"She says that about you."

"We all are, that's why she'll return. She can't find this any place else, right?"

"What's *this*?"

Melani pointed out the window, as if to say: *that.*

By the pond, Hostiles and Ju-Vee reunioners unfurled themselves from prone positions, blades of grass stuck to their faces, cracking knuckles and muttering obscenities. Many of them staggering straight towards the unkicked keg, others splashing into the pond among the Bodhi trees drowning heart-shaped leaves. The rescue dogs waded towards them, trailing tails in the water like snakes, their muzzles held aloft.

Maybe it was fatigue, or maybe it was coming down from whatever he'd taken that night, but the Hostel ethic struck Stone then (as it sometimes had before) as routine, commonplace, a rebellion and disavowal so scripted and paradigmatic that it reified that which it appeared to subvert. He realized that a raging resistance to life was the same as an ascetic withdrawal from it, that the resistance and withdrawal had to be combined with some kind of calculated participation, a modulation of Yes and No, or else all was static, bullshit, suicide. When Mariko left, he surmised, she took something with her, a vitality or spirit, something that connected them all, that made the thing work. Since then, Melani and the other Hostiles felt betrayed, he thought, concealing how much they missed her by accusing her of selling out and joining the "real world," the tainted, compromised outside world of parents, commerce, predation, conformity, love—Melanie and Stone had no idea how wrong they were until they watched the testimony.

As in her WebCam sessions, Mariko sat looking directly into the camera, but the bed in this case was some kind of bamboo mat on the floor, and instead of reclining languorously or posing with a sex-toy, she sat in a zazen posture, left foot on her right thigh, right foot on left thigh, spine straight, her hands forming a beautiful oval. Her piercings had been removed from her eyebrows, nose, lip. At first it looked like she was being held hostage, reading off instructions from an abductor out of the frame. As she spoke, a white veil fanned from her lips, which had no make-up and were brown and chapped, malnourished along with the rest of her slender frame, which now resembled Melani's.

Stone turned on the volume, Melani clutching his shoulder and somehow looking away from it and at it simultaneously.

"Not to continue my ways, not continue my behaviors, not to maintain what I think of as self or identity, but to retreat and become one with everything," Mariko said. "To kill not and cause no pain, to cause no desire, to forge no connections, but to rest and, in this spirit of rest, be like the wind in the trees. To live not in past or future, but now, the eternal now, which is always true."

Her eyes were downcast and her voice thinner, lacking its usual timbre, but at the same time she seemed resolute, not afraid or skittish like before.

"We say inner world or outer world or outside world, and create little worlds of separation, but the truth is there is just one big world, universe, soul. I know now that identities are just swinging doors within this limitless world."

She went on in this way, a way that really wasn't that shocking, Stone realized, had he been paying attention. It was like watching somebody commit suicide. He thought back to what she used to call the beautiful clean emptiness she yearned for during lawn duty sex, how she cried out in those orgasms not of pleasure but of non-being, of a time-out from something that she could never adhere to. Whether it was sex or drugs or sleep, she always said she wanted to leave no trace of herself, she wanted to burn herself out completely.

Since they'd caught it partially through the loop, the first words of her testimony were the last they heard: "My name is Mariko Damaare and, in my testimony, I want to give thanks to those who have helped me and forgive those who have contributed to my condition. This is the goal of our practice."

"Fuck does that mean?" Melani asked.

"Some religious shit, I don't know."

"That's not like her, I know her, what if she's on drugs or something?"

"She's always on drugs."

"You know what I mean. Maybe we can call the cops and they can...trace it or something."

"I don't want them here. That's the point. We can manage ourselves."

"What, then?" Melani asked. She swung out, facing him from the foot of the stairs. "So, we just don't do anything?"

Stone rubbed his eyes, looking back at her and just shrugged his shoulders.

Melani ran up the stairs and slammed the door to her room, her steps echoing to the bed where she and Mariko had sold themselves before. Stone moved the TV down next to the sculpture on the kitchen table to watch the video from the beginning, but before he started it up again he heard Farren shuffling down the balcony stairs and saw him appear in the doorway, holding the swinging door open.

He played with his nascent moustache, looking around the kitchen. "You cleaned good," he said. "I'd have helped."

"Did you see it?" Stone asked, motioning towards the TV.

"Parts. It was on when we were playing cards."

"What part did you see?"

"I don't remember, I was pretty fucked up."

"What did she say to you by the pond that day?" Stone asked.

"Who?"

Stone just looked at him.

"Nothing that warrants confession."

"I've asked you before. You and her by the pond that day, what did you say?"

"Just things, just talking about things."

"Since when did you two talk?" They faced each other across the room. Over Farren's shoulder he saw the Ju-Vee reunioners saying good-bye, kicking the stands off their cycles, revving their engines. They checked their watches and motioned vaguely goodbye to Stone's house with thrusts of their chins. The Hostel was emptying. Beyond them, horses trudged through the Amish fields, their muscles shining purple under the lambent sun.

"We both had decisions," Farren said. "The more we talked, the more it seemed like the same decision."

"You mean going back there?" Stone asked, pointing to the Amish compound. "Are you?"

"She was unhappy, she had been."

"Are you going back?"

Farren played with his moustache again and looked down. He was quiet for a minute, and then finally, after what appeared like much deliberation, he entered the room, the screen door thwapping behind him. He was tall and tan and with his hair whipped down he looked like a bored junkie. He flipped around a chair and sat with his elbows on its arms. In his periphery, Stone saw Melani creep down to the blind spot in the stairway, where Farren couldn't see her.

"What we figured," he said, "was that this here thing…it doesn't work, Stone. Maybe for a year it's fun. I had fun, I like you, you know that. But whatever we all fought against, or tried to prove sellin' drugs or doin' porn, at the end of the day it was fightin' against air." He picked up the sacred sculpture, holding it in his calloused carpenter's hands, inspecting its grooved construction.

"Is she coming back?" Stone asked.

"I doubt it." Farren looked Stone straight in the eye. "I can tell you this, once I leave, I'm not comin' back." He got up from the chair, scooting it back under the table and picked up Mariko's printed mantra from the puddle of Lysol.

"Peace Begins with Me," he recited. "She said that to me at the pond. Seems true. Begin with yourself, Stony, not against others. The harder you slam a door, the harder it swings back."

Farren left, roaming around the yard, thronged by the rescued dogs. He wasn't walking toward home, but Stone knew he would soon, and that Farren was right, that once he left, he would never come back. Melani cried, silently, not covering the tears that dribbled down her cheeks.

Stone opened two skunked beers and sat next to her on the narrow stairway.

She looked up at him, her lovely dark eyes wide and moist, sniffling, a splash of beer on her shirt. They kissed for the first time since Ju-Vee, since he told her he wasn't into girls, and as they kissed Stone closed his eyes, and through his mind a carousel of photos of the Hostel sequenced and fluttered and disappeared, as he realized for the last time that no matter what happened this hour or week or year, Melani too would leave him, as Farren and Mariko had before her, and that he would be consigned by fate to continue to rage in futile isolation against the world, surrounded by rescue dogs, Bodhi trees, and empty apartments, remembering the Hostel's noble experiment as a failure, while the little girls up the gravelly road jumped rope and chanted Amish songs together—but for now Stone and Melani, two orphans, nobody's children, left once again, hurt more than ever, kissed in the stairway, the kiss never moving beyond a kiss and not even lasting that long and meaning nothing afterwards. It was just nice to be together for that time then, for that instant, for that true Now, they both thought.

Multiverses

For Patrick Gallagher, my brother

On August 3rd, Denora friended me on Facebook.
On August 8th, followed me on Instagram and Twitter.
On August 14th, Denora invited me to join her LinkedIn network.
On August 15th, Denora winked at me on Match.
What makes these events notable—in other words, why you should care—is that Denora died in a scuba diving accident off the coast of Siesta Key that previous December. We were there with our seventeen-year old daughter, Brianna, who was competing in that year's American Swim-a-Thon™ 200-meter relay when her mother's corpse arrived at the coroner's. At that time, I was in the hotel bar, on my third margarita, writing the syllabus for my "Multiverses and Possible Worlds Theory" course.

Two months after the funeral, when things were starting to return to normal—me teaching physics at the Community College of Philadelphia and Brianna back attending United Friends High School—Brianna said we should keep Denora's social media profiles active.

"That's a thing now," she said. "Remember Jordyn Davies, her car accident after the prom? Her accounts are all still active, people tag her on Facebook at family gatherings, her sister posts Instagram pictures of her."

"Weird."

"You're weird," she said, removing leftovers cooked by neighbors and family from the freezer. "Virtual immortality. We can live on forever, like data. Mr. Brathis had us write a paper on it."

It made me proud but concerned to hear Brianna speak about matters like death. "I don't care what Mr. Brathis thinks, what would Mom think?" I asked. "And wouldn't we need her passwords and stuff?"

Brianna scoffed. "You're simple. I'll take care of it."

ଧଷ

So, therefore, the first question I asked myself was—who was pretending to be Denora? And why? Was it some glitch in the network, a system app error, some data transmission passing over through the multiverse? Some Yahooboy catfishing my deceased wife? But why her, and what could be done about it?

"I'll have to check on that one, hermano," said Jaime Hernandez, my neighbor and drinking companion. He wasn't technically a police officer but worked in digital forensics for the Police Department. We passed a bottle of Seagrams back and forth on Brianna's old swing set in the back yard, digging deep ruts into the soil with our heels. "In cases like this, the law hasn't caught up to technology, lo siento," he added.

My phone blinked and my breath caught, afraid it would be Denora's impersonator again, but it was Brianna, texting me that she had to close out the lifeguarding shift at the YMCA. It was the last week before she started college, so I texted back <b s8f> and handed my phone to Hernandez, clarifying, "So you can do something to find out about the…messages?"

"De nada." He leered at the phone's screen. "Any good shit on there, that chica I seen hangin' around?"

"She's just a student."

The student Hernandez referred to was named Annette Robinson. She was a widow, too, thirty-five, only five years younger than me. She currently worked as an Epic software trainer at Jefferson Hospital, but was in school to become a computer programmer. She was enrolled in my summer "Multiverses and Possible Worlds Theory" class, but after struggling with the initial units asked me to direct her towards a tutor. I offered to tutor her myself, since without Denora I was having increasing difficulty structuring my time effectively. I was drinking more, sleeping more, and working less. First, we met at the college library or Starbucks, but soon we were meeting for dinner, discussing our grief over glasses of wine, until we began sending private pictures and videos over various phone apps and ultimately having sexual relations one night at her condo. I resolved that it couldn't continue and that Brianna would never find out, until she did find out on the first day of August, discovering Annette's pictures and deleting them before throwing my phone at me and slamming her bedroom door.

"All right," Hernandez said, holding his hands in air apologetically. "All right. Whatever, professor." He groaned stepping from up from the swing's gully to the lawn, grinding his cigarette butt into the sand. "Let's take care of this now—and bring the whiskey."

……

"Interesting," Hernandez said, after examining my phone, browser history, modem, and router.

"Why? What's interesting?"

"'Member that ghost story about a girl in an empty house getting harassed by threatening calls, and when they check the phone records, the calls are coming from upstairs?"

"It's called *The Baby Sitter and the Man Upstairs*."

"Well, professor, we have the same situation here."

We crouched on the guest room floor beside the router and modem, Denora's clothes still stacked on the bed, boxes of her belongings on the floor.

"I don't know this stuff. What situation?"

"The phone number coming from the same house. Here, the messages are coming from the same house. Whoever is sending these messages is sending them from here, this network." He looked at me.

"Does that mean you think—

"I don't think anything, hermano, I just give the information."

I stood up, my knees creaking, looking out the darkened window towards the horizon. In the distance I saw the Schuylkill Expressway, the lights of cars flying past each other like stars, like souls swimming through the multiverse. I found it amazing there were so few accidents, a proof of God's existence.

"Unless," I said.

"Unless?"

"Never mind."

When Hernandez left, I went to Brianna's room, but all her devices, the laptop, the desktop, the Nexus tablet, the Kindle, the old iPhone, the older Samsung, were passcode or digital touch protected. On her desk was a calendar Denora and I had given her with each month featuring a picture of the three of us in a different American state. It had been our family goal to reach twenty states before Brianna started college at Lafayette University that fall, where she had declared a major in something called Digital Humanities. The calendar was the only non-digital thing in her room—everything else was automated, synced, on the cloud, gray or black, attached to a charging cord at all times.

The events marked on the calendar were typical for a seventeen-year old girl—typical in that every box was filled with writing. But I noticed there were small Xs on certain dates—August 3rd, August 8th, August 14th, August 15th, and thought back to Denora's messages and Hernandez's assertions that the messages were coming from this house. I called Brianna from the landline in the hallway but she didn't answer. I returned to her room and curled up on her unmade bed. It was past my bedtime.

I awoke to Brianna kicking me in the leg, shouting my name.

"What are you doing in here, Dad? Stop being weird."

I held out my hand. "I need to see your phone."

She backed away, tucking it into her pocket. "No, you really don't. That's creepy."

I was now sitting with legs crossed on her bed while she stood in the doorframe, as if she were the parent and I were the child. "Her profiles, you said you would take them down."

"We agreed to keep them up."

"I don't remember deciding that. You said you would take care of it."

She didn't say anything. You could see her ribs through her swimsuit and little cuts on her arms that she was trying to cover up with her YMCA towel. She'd started cutting again; it was a thing neither of us acknowledged.

"What are those Xs?" I asked, pointing to the calendar..

She covered her face with the towel. "I'm sorry," she mumbled.

"About what?" I was still on her bed. "I want to understand, baby."

"It was the pictures."

"What pictures?"

She took her phone out and shook it in front of me. "That other woman's pictures."

I cleared my throat and said, "What does that have to—"

"How can you just forget about Mom like that? When she... when it happened, down there, you said we would still be a family, that we would never forget her. Remember? You said that." Her voice was strained from crying. "I thought if I kept her alive..."

"Bri." I slid off the bed onto the carpet, cupping her chin to meet her eyes. "Bri—what did you do then? I need you to tell me. You're not in trouble."

She looked up at me. "It was for us."

৪৩ ০১

Later that fall Hernandez and I were drinking again on the swing set. I'd explained everything to him, that it was Brianna the whole time, sending the messages.

He nodded. "Terrible thing to lose a parent, never know how a kid'll react."

I played with the bottle's screw cap. "I broke it off with the student."

"Good plan."

We swung back and forth, breathing in the autumn smell. I heard the delicate crunch of fall leaves, a sound I'd always loved.

After Brianna left for school, the messages from Denora stopped—until October 9th, the anniversary of the day that Denora and I had met. On that day, Denora winked at me on Match, and I realized then that all that time she had been there, working through Brianna at first but working through digital networks now, from some other universe or world simulating or re-animating a lost love, between living and dead, gentle circuits crackling like synapses across multiverses. Maybe heaven was simply an infinite network of those you loved, I thought.

I accepted her friendship on Facebook.

I joined her LinkedIn network.

I followed her on Twitter and Instagram.

Finally, I winked at Denora on Match, texting in the prompt box with my clumsy thumbs <h@py anlvversry…..>.

Somewhere in Florida, An Angel Appeared

For Amanda Palmer

They slept on couches, park benches, a urine-stained recliner on the porch of a hospice in Valdosta, Georgia. Back seats, hatchbacks, haylofts, high school gyms, a treadmill somewhere in Florida. They did it for the band. Nallie once slept strapped to the top of the PunkVan, speeding down I-95 towards Richmond, waking up with a voice like a distorted blender but she killed that gig anyway. They did it for the music. Due to the nature and environmental hazards of where they slept, a variety of medical conditions occurred, including eczema, contact dermatitis, respiratory infections, and (as they entered their 30s), neck strain, herniated discs, sciatica. Bald Goran slept with Neeko, Neeko slept with Miriam, Miriam slept with a teenage fan in Lancaster, California, but didn't remember it until being informed by Nallie, who slept with the fan's sister, with Bald Goran, with Neeko, with anyone who desired her. They did it for the fans.

Somewhere in Florida, Nallie slept with Mariangelica, a stocky fourteen-year old with scars on her wrists and clunky shoes. Nallie woke up alone on a treadmill in the apartment complex gym, the message written in marker on the cracked linoleum reading "BUILDING 13, APT D. DONT KNOCK—M." She clasped her head and wandered out into the sunlight. Wearing a Lookout! Records t-shirt and black tights with unlaced Vans, she wandered through the apartment complex looking for the band.

There were polluted lakes, splintered sidewalks, overflowing dumpsters.

When she walked into Apartment D, an older chicana, who'd been sitting in a recliner as if it were a throne, hands flush with the chair arms, erupted from the chair and shook Nallie by the arms.

"You were the one with my Mariangelica last night?"

Nallie nodded, preparing for an assault.

"And you are the leader of the band?"

"I write the lyrics and sing," Nallie admitted.

"Then I owe you all my gratitude. I am Miss Maribella, Mariangelica's abuela." She hugged Nallie. "You saved my Mariangelica's life, you are an angel sent to us."

Nallie had never been called an angel, unless you counted being tucked in by her real mom as a little girl.

"Where is everyone?"

"Oh, they"—her voice lowered to a whisper— "everyone is fast asleep. You are all such nice young people."

"I've never heard that before," Nallie murmured. The apartment was filled with paintings of the Virgin Mary, rosaries, and candles. From the oven, a yeasty, homey smell wafted across the unit, sweet and spicey. At the age of thirty-four, Nallie had never used an oven.

The abuela took Nallie by the shoulders again and stood back with a broad smile, as if appraising her. "What you need, young lady, is sunshine. Come to the pool. When we return we can have cake with everyone, for my Mariangelica's Quinceañera."

She went out on the balcony and put blankets, sun tan lotion, and pool noodles into a Walmart bag.

Nallie peeked over towards the bedroom, wanting to locate the canvas knapsack containing their pills and syringes, the lighters and blades wrapped in socks. She felt panicky, something like circuitry spasms in her brain, twitching in her extremities, the first elements of withdrawal.

"I didn't know it was her birthday," Nallie whispered. She racked her brain for ways to get the knapsack without the old woman noticing. She didn't like other people knowing what she was up to, a trait that affected her attempts at sustained intimacy and actual adult life.

"She doesn't celebrate birthdays, but with you all here she will know it is special." The abuela grabbed Nallie by the arm and pulled her outside, saying "Come, come."

"It has been a very rough year for my Mariangelica," the abuela sighed. She and Nallie reclined on brown plastic lounge chairs, Nallie trying to relax. But the harder she tried the more her breath caught, the more her feet fidgeted. Cigarette butts dotted the bricks surrounding the pool and crumpled cans cluttered the shrubs under the gray palm trees. The "Pool Rules" sign had been vandalized with pictures of penises and the clock above it showed the wrong time.

"My Mariangelica was diagnosed with scoliosis. Do you know this?"

"That's why the shoes."

"For this the kids at school bullied her, and she fell into a sadness. She slept for many weeks, but then she started to learn your music and made her own lyrics, like yours, and she is better now. Because of you."

The abuela reached out and squeezed Nallie's hand. "Oh, you are so hot! Let's go take a swim."

"I can't swim."

The abuela laughed. "It's only four feet."

They waded into the water, the abuela performing complex geometries with her pool noodle, Nallie removing her T-shirt. The chlorine smell and sun on her limbs recalled a distant, forgotten memory of ice cream sandwiches and water balloon fights at Nickel Mines pool with her real family, when she was probably about six. She hadn't seen them in over twenty years.

The abuela swooshed over and took Nallie by the shoulder and hip, rotating her gently onto her back. She cooed into Nallie's ear, "You float. Keep your chin up. It is such beautiful sky, the clouds in Florida. Think of angels in the sky, and think too of angels all around us, in the swamps, in the subways, in the prisons, dealing drugs on the back streets. We need angels down here as much as up there. And you are such an angel." Nallie felt her body pushed through the water as she inhaled deeply, recalling family afternoons in her Little Mermaid swimsuit, her real mom bobbing her up and down in the shallow end, cooing "Wheeeeee! Wheeeee!"

Little Curly

I was first informed about our university's 25th reunion when Simone, my case manager at Soteria, shook me from my sleep and exclaimed, "You have a message, Mr. Memory." The staff called me that because, unlike most patients here, those with Alzheimer's or dementia, my memory remains intact. My first memory, for example, from when I was four, is of my dog being "put down" (what Professor Pankova had taught us was a *euphemism*) for biting a neighbor who had been pelting her with rocks.

I humped my walker to the lobby's obsolete desktop PC that froze because it needed more RAM, as I kept explaining to the Director, signing in with my password, /laika/, and squinted to read a forwarded message from Lane Fromick, my old college roommate and current hedge-fund millionaire. The body of the forwarded message was a formal invitation from the University Student Senate Reunion Committee (USSR-C), but in the direct message, which I saw was also CC'd to our other roommate that senior year, Ross Detweiler, it read: "Panky! Panky! Let's get her Dranky!!!!"

Simone, reading along, her dreads caressing my beard, whooped, "How exciting!" She said how great it would be to see old friends, but she didn't know how far apart we'd grown, how for the over two decades, while I had resided in Soteria, Ross and Lane had become executives, purchased houses, married, had children. I thought then, not of Lane or Ross (or even Nora), but of Professor Pankova, or Lenka, as she later asked me to call her. I wondered where she might be now, if she were still alive, if she had finally found the people who had forgotten her. I had never forgotten her, because she was the best teacher in my life—it wasn't what she'd taught in the classroom but what she taught me about empathy in that brief time we shared our despair in her home across from my senior-year frat house.

We'd been at 824 Bernitz for a week when we saw Professor Pankova, our Comp professor, for the first time in over three years. We were playing flip-cup on the roof with the girls we'd taken home from Hooligans (Nora was out of town). It was Lane who recognized her, drinking a bottle of something on her porch steps. Lane had received a call from the guy with the X up the street and had retreated to the roof's corner, motioning at the vapid giggling girls to cease their shrieking, and when he returned he was all like *"Shh shh yo yo,* I just saw our crazy first-year teacher."

The girls screeched at us to "Come back!" but we lowered ourselves on our elbows and crept to the edge of the roof. It was harder for me because of the swelling in my knees and elbows, the first, inconspicuous symptoms of my condition, but I persisted. We exclaimed *"Holy shit,"* laughing and using the TeleLens applications on our phones to see Professor Pankova (we only remembered her name later) more clearly. It was definitely her, we agreed. The grass plots on the three visible sides of her house were unmown; weeds sprang up on the walkway by her porch, twining upwards along the porch's chipped columns. Flowers drooped in pots with sad petals and resembled the weeds rising up from below to meet them, fornicating along the columns. In the corner of the porch was a bicycle with no rear tire, and a rocking chair facing the house. The screen door was torn and sort of on a tilt, held open by the lever at the top, allowing a little dog with curly, matted fur to run inside and out, yipping.

Her house, or more like *bungalow* (she'd taught us to always use vivid, descriptive terms), with its chipped paint and inebriated shingles, was bordered on both sides by frat houses, I believe Delta Zeta and Phi Kappa Phi, although it's hard to recall (I might be saying PKP because one of their pledges appeared at Soteria the other day saying he wanted to help "people with disabilities"). Like our place at 824, these frat houses were larger than the surrounding houses, lawns maintained by work crews hired from the local mushroom farms and the Dominican ghetto, driveways full of BMWs. That night the guys in D-Z were on their front lawn grilling shirtless, throwing footballs and chipping hacky-sacks. On the other side of the house, a bunch of PKP "little sisters" were dancing out on the wet cropped grass, gyrating to the techno music that I remember Nora used to like, their spectral forms lit by the confluence of the moon and the X-dealer's car up the street, which was parked with its blinkers on and the headlights illuminating the portion of the neighborhood from the PKP house to Professor Pankova's porch, set back farther from the street than the others, as if the house were a refuge.

Professor Pankova sat on the steps like a punished child, her knees pushed together and famous feet splayed out. She had on one of those gypsy dresses and sandals like I remembered she'd always worn to class, when we would hold our noses and point to her feet, which had callused toes and yellow nails, and make billowing aromatic motions to one another from our corner by the window that looked out on the quad where the girls tanned in April and May. Her face matched the dress, as if she were some kind of curly-haired gnome from a fairy tale or a little person from *The Wizard of Oz*, which she'd made us watch in class during the unit on Exile and Displacement.

No one remembered where she'd come from, some place that was part of the former USSR with a lot of consonants. Ross in particular remembered how enthusiastic she had been to introduce us to her culture and homeland, magnifying the country on Google Earth, playing popular records from home with unfamiliar instruments, passing around picnic baskets with baked goods we pretended to eat but hid in our bags and tossed into the trashcan as we left class.

"She was always so cheerful," Ross said. "It was weird."

I remember wondering whether she was just weird or if people from wherever she was from were just happier. On that night, however, she didn't appear cheerful. She drank from the bottle like a man, holding it by the tapered neck and chugging, looking up and down the street as cars passed, as if waiting for someone she knew wasn't coming.

"Panky-Panky!" Lane yelled. We poked him in the biceps and ribs, whispering for him to stop, but he laughed louder and repeated: "Professor Panky-Panky!"

She looked up and down the street again, and then over in a vague scan, pausing with the bottle by her chin, but didn't identify us. She pushed off the porch steps and limped inside, the barking dog twirling around her thick ankles, reminding me of how sick she had become by the end of that semester, how many times she had to cancel class or dismiss us early. (Those were the *pleasure* days that seem so distant now: 10 am parties, 3 pm hook-ups, waking up blacked-out the next day and telling our professors we were sick). She turned off the porch light and lowered the blinds. We returned to the girls and I used the random number generator I'd designed in Advanced Comp. Apps to determine who would be with who that night—who would be with *whom*, I imagined Professor Pankova correcting me in her squalid office with the picture of Laika harnessed into the Soviet space capsule.

The next night at Hooligans we discussed what to do about Professor Pankova. Lane and Ross, who'd both been on the wrestling team with me before my fatigue and swelling started, were bouncers there, and I was being paid in free meals and draft beer to improve the bar's network security. We were vaping out back by the garbage cans, talking to some of the waitresses from the Olive Garden next to Hooligans—across the parking lot from Soteria Community Recovery Center, where Professor Pankova had attempted to make us volunteer with her, and we'd gotten out of it by having the wrestling coach's assistant forge the volunteering slips. People over at the Recovery Center sat on benches or hunched over in wheelchairs, looking at the ground; some talked to themselves and walked with spasms and tics, even as the smoke blew over their porch and hung above them like a bell jar. They looked like figures in documentaries, gray and sepia-toned, slow moving, silent.

Our ideas about how to treat Professor Pankova depended on the grades we'd received and the memories of class we recalled. Lane, who would have lost his scholarship that year if she hadn't advocated for him before the academic standards committee, suggested we wait until she was not around and at least mow her lawn and weed-whack some of the shit on her porch. He didn't want to see her again, he said, but obviously she couldn't do it, and it was making our place look white trash.

I suggested inviting her to parties, getting her drunk, and earning invitations to see the inside of her house. This idea was partially motivated, I guess, by the humor of it, but I like to think—based on what happened later—that I felt a shard of kindness or compassion. However weird and exhilarating it had been the previous night to see her, by that night I only remembered her defeated, solitary form, slumped over with her curly hair sprouting like some sort of shrub. Ross, of course, still bore her a grudge because she had given him a D, which had resulted in him being unable to compete with the wrestling team for two semesters.

Since we couldn't agree on anything, we decided in the meantime that we would spy on her—this had become my area of expertise at the university, both officially and unofficially. I used a Wi-Fi Locator to obtain her wireless network and IP address, and, after breaking through her WAP2, set about accessing her browsing history and directory profiles.

I soon determined her network password to be /laika/, which Lane remembered was the name of the dog the Soviets had sent into space on *Sputnik*. Professor Pankova would often tear up while telling us how the dog had burned to ash in outer space, asking us to imagine its feelings of loneliness and betrayal, but we didn't know or care what these words referred to then. Pankova had seemed so much older than us when we were freshmen, but now we didn't fear her at all. We were beyond her pale powers, we realized, and so Ross and Lane wrestled and worked at Hooligans while Nora and I looked for a place in the city with an elevator for my knees, and the sparkling frats on both sides of her gray home crackled nightly with the hysterical vigor of hale youth as the hacking script I'd designed ran in the background of Professor Pankova's network, monitoring her activities.

II

We continued to see her nightly on the porch with her bottles. Sometimes she sat on the steps as she had the first time, bent and glazed-looking, gazing up and down the street as if she had just arrived from wherever she had come from years ago, as if the intervening years had not diminished her loneliness or estrangement. Other times, she sat on the inward-facing rocking chair and graded papers with an LED pen whose light haloed the paper's text. Or she played strange music and paced along the porch, looking up at the stars and moving her lips, the barking dog running inside and out. The grass grew, and the weeds and flowers reached towards one another, creating a kind of green sheath that concealed her from the neighborhood.

Even then I was learning the nature of exile, that it's not a geographical condition, but an emotional one. My degenerative and multiplying symptoms had ended my wrestling career and now radiated their effects to every other sector of my life: I couldn't play touch football at the shore, my classes had to be scheduled in special buildings with elevators, and even Nora at times evinced frustration, like that time we were at her sister's wedding and I was unable to dance. Everything I desired or had felt a part of was receding into mist.

Most nights now Ross and Lane would be gone until dawn, partying with the staff of Hooligans or with under-aged girls whose fake IDs they'd confiscate and return for blowjobs. Nora spent more and more time at her internship in the city, where she stayed with a cousin on the fourth-floor of an old building without elevators. It wasn't until I began inspecting Professor Pankova's posts on social network sites and forums that I learned she was experiencing the same emotions.

I stopped eating and started snorting schedule IV narcotics we received *gratis* from the wrestling program. I would take them and lay in bed propped up on pillows beside a dehumidifier to help with the inflammation and rashes that had begun appearing on my face and neck. From there I could see Professor Pankova's porch and perceive radiant sparks and color echoes splash-dancing from the two houses that surrounded it. Even when she wasn't on her porch, I could sometimes see her through the front window, hunched over her computer desk. I can't say for sure whether she looked *desperate* or *unhinged*, but those were the words she herself wrote on the forums and message boards and emails she sent to her sister and a man named Vlaz, who responded only once to say that she couldn't come home because he had married and there was no place for her.

She was so naive about online culture and technology that she was still actually using MSN and Yahoo! to perform search engine queries for "substance abuse," "depression," and "adjustment disorder." I followed her now on those sites from my rigged netbook, not for the sake of following her (as I pretended with the guys), but because sharing that space with my old professor *assuaged* (she would have circled that word in red with a smile) my feelings of loneliness and exile and what Nora on the phone said sounded like depression. In truth, I realized everything in life that had been promised me had been effaced, removed, destroyed.

The words that Professor Pankova typed as they scrolled across my screen seemed as though they could have come from me (even when they were in her native tongue and I needed to use the browser language extension I had refined to translate), and I remembered what she had said in class once about everybody making the same sounds through the same mouths when they cry. We had changed that to everyone making the same sounds when they cum—later proven to be untrue—but what she said about crying has held true, in my opinion, and believe me I've seen a lot of it here at Soteria over the past decades.

III

When our final classes were over, and Ross and Lane had gotten girlfriends and were rarely at the house on Bernitz, and Nora had left me for a guy she'd been fucking for months in her cousin's attic, and all the frats and sororities had their end-of-year parties, I remained propped in bed with my humidifier and netbook, observing the street's activities. The members of the other fraternity and sorority houses, those overgrown kids, placed appliances and trash on the sidewalk and just left them there; uniformed maintenance people and painters restored the houses to what they'd been before they'd been ruined by *pleasure*; and the grass surrounding Professor Pankova's house continued to grow, becoming almost tropical, and I almost expected to see the glistening scales of luxuriating rainbow snakes along the columns (reminding me of *One Hundred Years of Solitude*, which she'd assigned and I'd barely skimmed)—anyway, it was then, after my advisor informed me that my health petition had been denied and I would have to graduate in the summer, that I took the metro bus with the underprivileged, non-college-affiliated minorities to Hooligans to see Ross and Lane for the first time in weeks.

They were working the door but it was a quiet Monday night, so we talked about what they were doing that summer, where the wrestling team had placed, the jobs and five-digit bonuses they had landed through Career Services. None of us drank because they were on shift, and alcohol was contraindicated with the NSAIDs I'd been prescribed for the condition nobody ever diagnosed.

When that night's band arrived, Ross and Lane carted in the amps and drums, and I limped to the corner booth and watched a baseball game. I experienced a sensation that had become increasingly common for me, the sensation that, even at my young age, I was seeing most of my past and future fade. I would never again slide into second or run down a fly ball; I would never again tailgate, killing kegs and fighting opponents' fans; I would never have a girlfriend like that guy on the TV behind home plate, whose girlfriend looked at him the way Nora used to look at me. I felt my stomach drop and a sense of great emptiness and floating disconnection—I didn't want my degree in Computer Design, I didn't want to get back with Nora, I couldn't think of one thing I desired.

I hobbled outside, ignoring Ross and Lane's puzzled looks. I sat on a bench and stared at the people outside of Soteria. I told myself: "Think of them as people"; I told myself: "Think of them as you." I looked at them and forced a smile. Nobody smiled back; they only looked at me as if interpreting a gesture from an alien culture. A woman with skin like plastic bags holding her dentures in a palsied grip motioned for me to come sit next to her. I walked over, massaging my gimpy right knee, and saw Ross and Lane come outside and light up, winking at me as if I were playing some kind of practical joke.

Then I saw her, Professor Pankova, as I approached the Center and entered the circle of invalids; I saw her through the slats in the blind of one window, wearing her customary gypsy dress, her stubby arms flying apart as she expressed something, her face partly obscured by her curly hair. For the first time, I opened the door and entered Soteria. There was no air-conditioning, only two oscillating fans at distant corners. Everything looked rundown—the furniture was second-hand, the carpet was stained and rubbed bare, the air was stale with sweat and the smells of older bodies. Residents sat on couches and folding chairs in a U-shape around Professor Pankova, just as we had in our first-year class. Like those spoiled, selfish children we had been, the residents also seemed to disregard her passion, looking at the floor, chewing their lips, cracking knuckles, the same way that we passed notes, texted our girls, or gazed out at the quad. I closed the door softly behind me so it wouldn't bang and shuffled to the back of the room.

"This is what I try to say," Pankova was saying in her still choppy, child-like accent and foreign syntax. She stood beside one of those old cathode-ray tube television sets with a VCR tray. There was a paused image from *Homeward Bound*, the two dogs and cat that I recognized from childhood. She continued: "No matter how much you... *flounder* alone, no matter how much you feel was taken from you, or how lost and alone you are, things can be in reverse. I mean, change. All day, things change."

A man wearing a stained tracksuit snorted, shaking his head in disbelief. She stopped and addressed him. "Do not shake your head like that Mr. Tenly, like you are given up," she said. "I repeat: every day provides us with opportunity to get back lost things, to return to our homes like these animals. Anyone can be loved, any place can be home: you all deserve this. We deserve this."

She re-started the movie and took quick little steps to a chair next to the TV, scanning the audience with a puzzled smile. She paused when she saw me, continuing to scan around, aiming the smile the way she aimed her eyes when she spoke, and then she looked directly back at me and waved by bunching her fingers into a fist and flexing it. She motioned for one of the other volunteers to get me a chair, and I sat in the back and watched until the end of the movie.

Afterwards, she walked up to me. She only came up to my chin and smelled vaguely of broth. "Hello there, Mr. Sonsteim," she said

"Professor," I replied.

"Lenka. You call me Lenka now." She sat down on a seat next to me, her knee butting against mine. I winced. "Is it knee that is in pain?" she asked.

"It's nothing," I said. It was hard to explain.

"I drive you home," she said. "I know you are neighbor, you shy fellow. I keep waiting for you to visit." She winked at me. "And now you visit and explain. This is what it is to be a neighbor, to share, to overcome loneliness." She grabbed her keys and folded her fluffy coat over her forearm. She looked at me again and said, "It has been so long between the two of us!"

When we arrived at 827 Bernitz she warmed up goulash and opened a bottle of wine, placing it on a kitchen table covered with envelopes marked by the postal service as "Address Not Found."

"I do not entertain," she explained. I was bent down on the floor playing with the little dog, which kept yipping and licking me, until my knees hurt too much and I leaned against the wall, holding the spastic thing up against my lap. She looked up from the stove and frowned, saying, "Is your knee?" She pointed to the bottle on the table, a cheap $10 Burgundy. "Would wine help?"

I shook my head. "I can't drink," I said. "Pills." I noticed I pointed at my head like the pills were there.

"And they are working?"

I struggled up from the floor and sat at the table. She ladled the goulash out into two wooden plates and brought them to the table.

"Pain all over," she said, piling the unopened letters onto an empty chair and placing the two plates before us. "I know of it, it is always different place, pain, but the same still." She squinted her eyes and smiled.

"It feels like, when I tell people, they don't really want to know."

"That is true of many things, no?" she asked. "You can tell me; you will always be my student."

I shrugged.

I told her about Nora, and Ross and Lane, and how everyone had left me. She listened, nodding occasionally and looking straight at me, which everyone else in my life had stopped doing. When I finished, she hugged me and said, "When life takes friends from us, life gives us new friends back."

After dinner she asked if I wanted to sit on the porch with her. She pointed at the little curly-haired dog and said, "I call him Toto," and giggled. I stood on the porch steps with her as she finished the bottle in the rocking chair. The street was quiet, the houses dark, the driveways empty.

"Johnny (it sounded like *zhonniez*), you do technology, no?" She removed a flip-phone from her pocket.

I shrugged to indicate yes.

"Is it possible," she said, petting Toto, "for service to not work, that when I call people or *text message*, as you students say, nobody receives them?"

"It depends."

"This will sound silly, but my phone, I wonder if it works? Nobody responds to my texts or calls. Is it possible they do not get them?" She drank from the bottle and handed me her phone. "Could you look and see?"

I looked at her phone's sent log, seeing hundreds of text and calls to contacts named Vladimir, Svetlana, Marina, Babushka. "It looks like they've been sent," I said, handing it back. "Sometimes people change numbers or the network goes down," I added, feeling bad about lying.

"You're a kind boy," she said, after a long pause. "I think that they have forgotten. Promise, never forget me. You will live long, happy life, and I want you to always remember me." She giggled. "Tell your grandkids about your silly college English teacher."

As those nights between us became more and more frequent, we began to develop an actual friendship. We started a book club, "just for two," she joked, and at least two or three times a week we would eat together, either her cooking something or me ordering in. I moved in the bookshelves that Ross and Lane no longer used and organized her books into different subjects, like Russian literature, American literature, poetry, and psychology. When my lease on 824 Bernitz expired in May, I moved into an empty bedroom in Pankova's house.

While I still talked to Lenka at dinner or on the porch, for the most part I laid in bed for months, watching as the new semester began and 824 was rented by a new iteration of frat boys, acting out the same rooftop drug experiments and sexual games I used to participate in. I was full of self-pity, something I couldn't prevent Lenka from noticing.

One night on the porch, she asked, her voice quiet, looking at the floor, "Did class volunteer?"

"What class?"

She waved her hands (she wasn't drinking that night; I had noticed her drinking less and less) and said, "It is no thing, I just... you remember in our class when I asked you all to volunteer? At Soteria? And you all gave slips saying you did?"

I didn't say anything. I couldn't determine whether lying to her now or admitting that we had all lied to her then was worse.

"It is ok, I just wondered," she said. "I bring it up because volunteering, Johnny, I do not mean to force you, but it helps. You meet people. You get out of your room. You stop thinking of self. It is a thing that just happens."

I didn't volunteer, not then. I was too consumed with the direction my life had taken. I returned to my bedroom, my netbook, my humidifier, watching the colored world outside the window, taking increasing amounts of narcotics. After a year, my symptoms had become so serious that I couldn't take care of myself, and, despite Lenka's protestations that she could take care of me, I admitted myself into Soteria as a resident. She disappeared six months later, but I was the only one who seemed to notice.

I didn't go to the reunion and I never talked to Lane again. Those were different times, and I've matured enough to know now that I can't recover them. The best I could do, I realized, was learn to embrace this new life at Soteria. Sometimes, when my symptoms are flaring up and all I want to do is lay in bed, I remember Professor Pankova's message of hope, of how things can change, how people can be helped. There are certificates in my room commemorating me as "Teacher of the Month" for the work I do teaching other residents how to use search engines, how to share their feelings on message boards and forums, and, most importantly, how to use electronic mail to communicate with friends and family. At times, when they ask me why nobody responds to their electronic mails, just like Professor Pankova asked me why nobody responded to her texts decades before, I think of how Laika, or "Little Curly," as Professor Pankova once told us the dog was nicknamed, must have felt as she ascended above the atmosphere, condemned to burn alone among the stars and cosmic residue, barking in mute space "I'm hurt and alone," swirling among the falcate galaxies.

My Friend Joe

The plumber arrived after midnight. Tugce could only guess at the functions of the equipment he lugged up the sidewalk—coily hoses, floppy saws, a round tubular thing that reminded her of R2-D2, from *Star Wars,* her favorite American movie. She stood at the window in her rented cap and gown, looking down as the man in the "Make America Great Again" hat entered the building.

The rest of the dorm was empty, the other international students out celebrating, but Tugce had remained behind, intent on reflecting on all she'd learned in America in preparation for her graduation speech tomorrow—except all she did was practice smiling in her cap and gown, playing with the cap's little tassel so that it covered a pimple.

Tugce heard the plumber's heavy steps and the scraping of his tools against her bedroom door. There was some kind of podcast blaring from his person, the broadcaster's voice shrill and insistent, screaming "Zero tolerance is the only justice!" The plumber entered the bathroom and started banging, flushing and re-flushing the toilet, making a drilling sound that reminded her of the dentist.

Tugce had told her dormmates she wanted to stay home to write her speech, but in actuality she was afraid of putting herself a situation where there would be alcohol. On campus, people assumed she abstained for cultural or religious reasons, but what really concerned her was how much she *loved* it. This was the subject she wanted to address in her speech, but she was concerned about publicly admitting to alcoholism. She worried that she was an alcoholic even though she didn't drink that much, but rather because her behavior changed and she did things that she either was ashamed of the next day or didn't remember at all. How could she talk about it without mentioning specifics?

A crash came from the bathroom. Tugce removed the cap and gown and put on a New Mexico State University hoodie. She looked down the hallway and called out, her voice accented and mild, "Mister?" She was cautious, but as a nurse she had been trained to intervene in potentially dangerous situations.

She entered the bathroom with her medic kit and rushed to the man's side, squatting next to him. He was rolled up in a fetal position on the tiled floor, his temple bruised, his nose bleeding. There was blood on the lid of the toilet. He lifted himself up on one arm, took a drink from a flask, and grimaced. "Are you an angel?" he joked.

"I am Tugce Adaba Alihpiri. I'm a nurse?" She didn't know why she intonated it as a question.

"Welcome to America," he said. "I'm Joe. A good American name."

Bending over beside him, she could smell whiskey, cigarettes, and hemorrhoid cream. She sopped up the blood on his face with a handful of cotton gauze squares, gently plugging the last one in his right nostril, and then palpated his temple. He had a coarse, puffy face, with burst capillaries under his eyes and along his nose and lips.

The man on the radio screamed, "They want us to become a shithole country like where they came from!"

Tugce asked him to turn off the radio, saying she needed to concentrate.

He scrutinized her face but she focused on treating his wound, and when glancing at him showed a visceral sincerity and dedication to task that had, in addition to her perfect GPA, resulted in her being named the nursing cohort's valedictorian.

"I guess you're in charge," he said, grabbing his phone with the American flag case and turning off the audio. "You from Iraq?"

"Did you ever hear the joke about Turkey?" Tugce asked, her warm brown eyes sparkling. "Ok, so a guy says 'I'm so Hungary I could eat a Turkey.' It's funnier if you see the words."

Joe cleared his throat and said, "It goes 'I was *Hungary* so *Iran* to the fridge to get some *Turkey* but there was *Greece* on it and I was like, there's *Norway* I can eat that.'"

"That *is* funnier," she exclaimed.

Joe tried to stand up but he swayed, and Tugce guided him to the toilet seat. She bent over and lifted up his chin, making eye contact. "Sit here and rest. I am going to give my speech for you." She hurried back to her room and put her cap and gown back on.

"So, okay," Tugce said, stepping onto the side of the bathtub and standing above him. She cleared her throat. She looked American, but was that just because America didn't look like America anymore? She read from the phone in her left hand. "In summary, then," she began.

"Summation," Joe said gently, his hands folded in his lap. He met her eyes. "It's 'in summation.'"

She stroked some keys on her phone and nodded. "In summation, then." She giggled and made a goofy face. "Okay, in summation, all of us graduates here have one thing to be proud of: that we persevered. There were bad times, times when we wanted to give up, when we missed home, but in the end we are here. For me, the best times were the worst times, you say *rock bottom* I believe in America, here, our new home. I believe that without hitting rock bottom, we can't ascend to the top of the mountain."

"That's good," Joe said. "Rock bottom part."

"That's the end anyway," Tugce said. She sat down on the bathtub's lid.

"Maybe tonight is my rock bottom," Joe whispered. He didn't say anything more, he didn't cry or put his head in his hands or dramatically throw the flask away. He just sat there, playing with his fingers.

"If it's rock bottom, then you should be so happy. There is nowhere to go but better."

"Up," Joe said.

"Up, then." Tugce smiled, her teeth slanted but clean. "Even better." They sat that way until dawn, him penitent on the toilet, his scarred hands like slabs of ham. Tugce watched him openly, observing his tremors, his flushed face, his humped back. And she knew then what she could talk about in her speech without giving herself away.

Meran

For MLC

"Then at least tell me what the doctors say," Meran had said. She was alone in the darkened apartment, splayed between blankets and heating pads, propped up by Hello Kitty pillows. Aromatherapy candles illuminated crumpled tissues, pill bottles, and insurance forms on the table where I used to snort cocaine and play drinking games.

I felt domesticated, my life a numb vector between our apartment and the Recovery Lodge just down the road. In those days I was annoyed, thinking of Meran whining on the couch, researching symptoms on her iPad; I was resentful that her vague illness had diminished my life's promised fun, distracting me from proximate pleasures; I was ashamed when I lied about working in order to go see Vicka (like I had earlier that day). I used to believe that this was justified, but now I realize what Meran knew all along—that there is no grace like serving, and no betrayal like neglect.

Meran was thirty-two and I was twenty-three then, but her illness made her look younger, pale and elfin, her features adolescent. While her body had wilted and whitened, her slender face had swelled from prednisone. There was a U-shaped rash under her nose caused by her constantly crying and blowing her nose, which had begun to bleed a few weeks before. Our roles had reversed from the time when we had first met at my older sister's wedding a year before (they had been in Student Council together in high school), from the time when I'd stagger from bars or parties to her place with my bloody and swollen face, which she'd tend to before putting me on the couch with water and aspirin.

Meran skeeved my apartment because it was "gross": the dishes gobbed with cheese and stacked in the sink, the soiled cushions on the couch, the smell of cigarettes and beer, semen stains on my deflated air mattress. Unwashed towels hung over the windows and clothes lay in corners.

The backyard plot was strewn with ripped trash bags, overflowing green bins of Keystone Ice, pizza boxes molded into Cubist shapes by the rain. I was unemployed at the time and slept all day, only awakening to texts from Meran with little sunshine emoticons accompanied by messages like "Get Up Mattie!" and "It's a beautiful day!"

I never thought of these behaviors or decisions as Activities of Daily Living, or ADLs as they are termed at the Recovery Lodge. For months Meran had suggested I get a job at the Recovery Lodge as a Human Health Aide, which I ignored until I got my second DUI and my probation officer demanded that I either become employed or enter rehab again. She helped me get a job there, where I'd assist clients with their ADLs. Most clients had just been released from mental hospitals, and most of the staff were work-release probates or divorced alcoholics.

Together, the Recovery Lodge clients and I learned how to clean ovens, water plants, request money orders, avoid the evils of preservatives. We watched YouTube videos about "How to Tie Ties" and attended GED preparation meetings. On Saturday mornings we cleaned—usually with me using the vacuum, and the clients spraying Lysol on the counters and Febreze on the furniture. On Monday and Wednesday evenings I took them to AA and NA meetings on Lispert Street. I sat in the back, scrolling Plenty of Fish, ignoring the stories of recovery.

On Saturday afternoons, we all convened at the office for a community meal. The clients brought whatever they could make or purchase, small things like diet soda or crackers, while Meran taught me how to bake casseroles, peel potatoes, place the silverware in the proper arrangement. I had never before prepared anything aside from boiled pasta or burned frozen pizza. When we all sat down at the two plastic tables pushed together to eat, Meran served everyone and sat back, not eating anything herself, asking every person to tell the group about One Good Thing that had happened that week. Whenever she asked me, I said her, and she blushed.

Meran moved into my apartment about six months prior to that night—I think of it as the last night, at least the last night in spirit. With a kerchief tied around her flowing hair, she scrubbed the linoleum in the bathroom and kitchen, and removed and washed the towels in the windows, folded the towels in the bathroom closet and arranged the windows with tulips and peonies. I replaced my air mattress with a Queen-sized bed from Target and junked my desk from IKEA for a maple one her grandfather had built. For the first time in my life, I slept regular hours, and stopped drinking and getting high. We vacationed at the shore and ate at restaurants requiring reservations; Meran giggled with her bright green eyes every time the manager made me wear a rented blazer. I learned what it's like to share life with another person, to feel connected—that safe feeling I had never experienced before or since, knowing that whatever happened to me, with Meran I wouldn't relapse, I wouldn't go back to using.

One time we were on the couch watching Lost on a rainy Saturday. I asked her the question that had been on my mind since we'd met, "Why are you here? You could be with anyone. Not some junkie loser."

"Just hush," she said. "Enjoy yourself, enjoy us, being here now."

"So I'm like your project?" I asked.

She rolled over so her eyes were looking up from my lap, folding her strong tan arms around my neck. She looked at me seriously and said, "I pick you. It's my decision. You can hate yourself, but I love you, and you don't have any right to ask me about it."

She pulled my face down to kiss her, biting my lip before letting go, and turned towards the TV and said, "Put on the next episode, it's the one I was telling you about, the one with the Smoke Monster."

I hid the remote under the cushion. "You'll have to earn it," I said, my voice suggestive.

She turned back towards me, her voice sarcastic, asking, "What are you thinking?"

"Take care of the kid," I said, gesturing towards my pants.

"You mean this guy?" she asked, rubbing her palm softly over my crotch. "Has he been feeling neglected?"

I nodded, hardening, leaning back on the couch as she shifted onto her knees and unzipped my jeans.

"Perv," she said, giggling. "He is a cute little guy, though."

It was the happiest time in my life, and it lasted less than six months before she became sick—something the monster in me blamed her for, no matter how much I tried to be good.

⚭

My eyes adjusted to the darkened room, where it seemed like midnight even though it was only seven. The National Geographic Channel was broadcasting something about flowers, but Meran had muted the volume because she claimed the noise worsened her migraines. Outside, the others had finished off the grill and now threw Frisbees at buckets, red Dixie cups of Yuengling by their feet.

"Nothing's wrong with you," I said, answering her question. I directed a clownish expression at her that used to make her laugh before everything bad began: the diseases, my cheating, the miscarriage, the written warnings I received from the Recovery Lodge for stealing pills.

She blew her nose and said, "That's the point. You won't talk about it, you won't say the names of the diseases, you're just pretending that this isn't happening." She stuffed the used Kleenex into a CVS bag full of them, not looking at me. Her cat crouched on the couch's arm, peering at the wallpaper's design.

"You know something's wrong," she persisted. "Look at me and tell me nothing's wrong. Tell me what I have. Just share this with me, that's all I'm asking. We both know what's happening."

I knew some of the names of the diseases, but I didn't like to discuss it. I didn't know why she always wanted to, and changed the subject.

"Want me to go get some tulips?"

"Tulips smell too strong, they're not good for my head. I've told you that."

"Maybe those chocolate things? You should treat yourself. It'll get your mind off it."

"What's it?" she asked. "Me being sick? Having crazy diseases nobody's ever heard of and people all think I'm just whining and my own boyfriend can't even be on my side?"

Her declining health was the only thing she talked about anymore. She cringed forward, motioning with her one free arm (the other constrained by her heart monitor) around the emptied room, sliding the iPad onto the ground beside the rumpled CVS bag. My Wii controllers and old drug paraphernalia were packed in shoeboxes she'd stacked in the closet. I sat on the rocking chair her grandmother had bequeathed to her when Meran announced her pregnancy at two months, the rocking making my buzz return as I slid the chair towards the couch.

"Hush, babe," I said, taking out the meds I'd hooked from the office. "'Just be here with me."

I moved the bag with medications onto the table, helplessly holding the pills out to Meran like sacraments.

Meran leaned forward, holding her stomach, two translucent strands of hair resting on her chapped lips. She inspected the pills, separating the chalky white painkillers, Percocet, Vicodin, and Talwin, from the Xanax footballs and cobalt Ambiens. She pointed at the Vicodin.

"I can't swallow those," she said. "Instead of actually understanding, you just steal meds to shut me up."

"It's just that I don't want to see you in pain."

"It's not the pain, Mattie, it's that it doesn't work. That's why it happened, the accident. It's my stomach, and everything down there, y'know." She sniffed and grabbed a tissue. "You're never here anymore. Only if you're feeling guilty. Even if you're here you're not really here. I can tell, I'm not stupid. This shit hasn't affected my brain yet."

"I have to work, since you can't."

"Oh right, I forgot everything's my fault because I can't work. You don't think I want to work? You think I want to whine in the dark taking pills all day? Maybe that's what you want but I have a life and values and things to offer, Mattie. This is bullshit. Everyone pretends to care until it's inconvenient. It's like I'm invisible. Just leave, give yourself a break." She folded a pillow over her head and whipped back onto the couch, her face pressed into the cushions.

"Close the window," she mumbled. "I can't stand hearing those people laughing."

I was chewing gum to hide the smell of alcohol, and tossed my hoodie on the windowsill so she couldn't smell smoke on it. From the window I saw them: it seemed the entire neighborhood was walking in sandals towards the community pool, beach towels slung over their shoulders or tied around their waists. The pool was between the playground and the apartment complex's fitness center (the triad advertised as the "Fun Zone" by the real estate company). It was situated as a sort of buffer between the condos and townhouses on our side of the rise—populated by college students and young unmarried couples—and the county-subsidized studio units of the Recovery Lodge on the lower side of the hill, where the constant floods turned the lawn a perpetual brown. The design was fucked up; often you couldn't tell who was in recovery and who was not.

Vicka stood on the diving board, her blonde hair swaying in the wind, laughing with her head bent back and eyes closed. She wore a commercial smile that turned serious as she sloped her lean body down, cutting through the pool's surface and gliding underwater until she emerged on the other side, elbow on the edge. Meran was either crying or moaning in pain, and I returned to sit on the couch without touching her. I was high and slightly buzzed from the three tequila shots and was paranoid that I smelled like Vicka's strawberry conditioner. I did not know how things had started with Vicka and did not know how to end things with her; it was a thing I simply pretended was happening yet had no meaning, certainly nothing to do with Meran's illnesses or inability to function sexually.

"Mattie?" Meran whispered.

I rubbed her through a blanket, her hip bones jutting out.

"Sorry I was a bitch," she said.

I moved closer and rubbed her body some more, somewhere around her shoulders or neck. She didn't respond. I rubbed her now the way I rubbed my dog as a boy, completely unlike the way I used to caress her.

"You don't need to pretend you love me," Meran said, mumbling into the pillows.

"Don't talk," I said, stroking her hair and feeling her forehead. "Get some sleep."

"Will you be here tonight?"

I told her I needed to work the overnight shift, but would only be a minute away if she needed me.

"Is Vicka working too?" she asked.

"I don't know," I lied. "Doesn't matter, I have GED stuff."

She was quiet for a minute, one of those periods of silence where you just know things are fucked, that silence that says more than words. "Return the meds," she said, "the Lodge needs them more than me. I can deal."

That evening, after Meran fell asleep I wiped away her tears and checked the heart monitor for proper functioning. I cradled her body under one arm and tucked her into the bed we used to share, making sure she was on her right side so her heart wasn't pressed down. I checked that the thermostat was set to eighty-two, as her doctors had ordered.

Those were the days with Meran I remember, when I think of her now, a decade later. It's a story I don't usually tell because it makes me look like an asshole, there's no getting around it. At the same time, it reminds me of Meran's heart—not her diseased heart, too sluggish to pump blood to her depleted body, but her soul's heart. Of all those who'd worked at the Recovery Lodge in those days, she was the only one who had started and ended her involvement as a volunteer, the only one who didn't steal meds from patients. She was the only one who forwarded the office number to her own phone even when she was sleeping or too ill to intervene, just so she would know how everyone was. When I think of Meran's heart I think of the possibilities of the human heart, those deep, curious passions I never felt except with her.

I got the crayons and construction paper and scissors that Meran had used as an occupational therapist and took them out on the roof via the fire escape, along with some other things I'd gathered. From there you could see over the Fun Zone down to the Recovery Lodge, which consisted of roughly twenty-five identical brown brick units. I located Meran's browser history on her iPad, found bookmarked sites and apps for clinics and 501(c)(3) organizations and FAQs for disease names that I had heard her mention or had seen on insurance forms. I drew a cartoon picture of Meran as a little girl with black pigtails and puffy cartoonish hands and feet and described the conditions in little text-clouds with arrows pointing to the parts of the body involved ("Meran's heart has an arrhythmia that causes dehydration and fatigue") and on the other side I drew that same reversed body with different text-clouds ("Meran's heart is full of love").

I cut shards of pink paper and folded them into hearts like Mrs. Wendelsam taught us in third grade, and then texted Vicka

I titled my art project "What's Wrong with Meran/What's Right with Meran" and left it beside her bed (I no longer considered it "our" bed), hoping it would make her happy or provide a moment's relief, while already feeling on her cheeks the night sweats that would soak the covers in two hours.

And it did help for a while, she told me once later, before it didn't matter anymore.

₧₨

There is no language for a confession or expression of guilt that doesn't at the same time implicitly ask for forgiveness, even if the person betrayed is absent. The language I'm using is insufficient to convey the tragedy of Meran's isolation and the forfeiture of my opportunity to save her life the way she had, for a while, saved mine. What Meran had taught me about the nature of love and sacrifice and the ethos of the gift—when you give without considering compensation—was the opposite of the way I lived. The latter reminded me of what Mr. Spomane and the counselors said repeatedly about substances: that we addicts used them because the substances required nothing from us.

₧₨

After I left her, I talked to Meran only once more before she died. I was back in the same rehab again. The people there were the same people who had been there, in and out, over the past decade. My family had long since given up on me and my friends were all dead or in other rehabs. I spent my days curled up on the couch alone. I knew that I had been at fault, that I had allowed my thoughts about what my life should be like to distract me from the truth and reality of that life.

Our counselor, Mr. Spomane, liked to say that you do something before you think of something, and the doing creates the emotion. That's the opposite from how we normally conceive of how emotions work. This is why we felt better praying to a God we didn't believe in, he said; the behavior created the emotion. What I prayed was that I could have ignored Vicka and my idealized visions of fun, that I wouldn't have thought about Meran's illness as being unfair, and that I had just acted with Meran the same way that I did with my clients. I should have helped her with her ADLs, I should have listened, I should

85

have left our connection unsevered. I wanted to tell her this, to apologize. I got my chance when she showed up unannounced at the rehab unit with her fiancée. That was two years ago.

A strange man wheeled her in, clearing a spot in front of the soiled couch I was lying on. Meran looked even frailer than before, with some kind of port distending from her abdomen, her legs so palsied that it was like half her body was in a fetal position. But there was still an aura or a spark—I think I loved her again then, but I might just think that now, looking back, trying to be a good person. I stumbled up from the couch, repeating Meran's name in a weird cadence, hugging her gently in the chair, barely touching her, as if she might crack if held too tight.

"You look good," I said.

She smirked. "We're past all that, Mattie. I know what I look like."

Her teeth were yellow and her gums splotched with blood. She had what she identified as a PICC line in a vein in her arm, which was connected to a fluid container taped to the wheelchair. Even though it was summer, she was wearing a hoodie and sweatpants with heavy exercise socks. I noticed that her nails, which had always been manicured, were chewed up and grey, as if they weren't part of her anymore, like old gloves.

"Well it's not like I'm model of the year either," I joked. I was wearing a tracksuit from Goodwill that I hated but which absorbed my sweat and concealed my gut. She smiled and looked over at the man beside her. He was taller and older. They clenched hands. He was completely bald and had one of those tracheotomy things from smoking inserted into his throat.

He gave me a thumbs-up and then kissed her on the cheek.

"Mattie?" Meran paused. "Mattie, this is Gottfried, we're getting married next week. Nothing big, just family, friends, a civil union thing, but there will be food and dancing and stuff for people who can do that. You should come."

"Next week?" I said.

"Well, we better do it soon before we're dead," she said, looking up at Gottfried with a smile. He caressed her PICC line, ensuring it stayed inserted.

"We met at a recovery meeting," Gottfried said, as if someone had asked. "Nice meeting you. I figure I'll give you two some time alone."

He bent down and kissed Meran. "Let me know when you need me," he whispered.

Meran gave him one of those smiles that looks like a wince. She rotated her wheelchair so she was sitting closer to me. We tangled our fingers together.

"I was an asshole," I said. "I should have stayed, been there for you." I paused. "I deserve to rot in this place."

"You were," she agreed. "That doesn't mean you still are. You're young, Mattie, you have time, you have life. That's all you need to recover."

"I'm sorry."

"I don't hate you," she said. "That was a hard time for a lot of people, I lost a lot of friends. The way to tell who your friends are is to get sick, believe me."

We traced each other's fingers, in a sort of trance. Meran looked up at me with concern but also with a smile, a weak smile that seemed to contain special knowledge.

"I don't blame you Mattie, you just couldn't handle it," she finally whispered in my ear, before motioning across the room to Gottfried. "Please come to the wedding."

I went to the rec room, signed out scissors and the markers that some of us huffed, and asked for construction paper from one of the orderlies.

"What for?" he asked.

"A wedding card," I said.

"For fuck's sake," he said.

I made the same card as I did that last night with Meran, but only used one side this time, focusing on what was right about her, what I loved about her, what I was sorry for. The only way to truly apologize, I figured, would be to ensure that Meran knew how I'd never forgotten her, how nobody had, how she had changed everyone's life for the better. I wrote all that and finished the card, and wrote Meran a letter of confession, signing it "Love Always" and folded it inside the card. The next day a counselor who was close to me in size brought in one of his suits for me to wear, and the other patients in rehab pitched in money so I could purchase a $20 gift card for Starbucks as a wedding gift.

I'd just received a special pass to leave the unit when Gottfried called the nurse's office two days before the wedding, his robotic voice informing me that Meran was dead. The head nurse only let me listen to the message twice before she deleted it. I didn't attend the funeral but used my pass for the memorial, where only Gottfried recognized me. He shook my hand weakly and said, "She'd be glad you're here. I'll leave you to pay your respects."

As I waited in line, my heart palpitating and hands trembling, I looked with an odd kind of reverence at the picture of her on the mantle over the coffin. She was standing in the Fun Zone surrounded by clients from the Recovery Lodge—standing in the middle of the group, smaller than all of those who huddled over her in awkward embraces. Her gummy smile was bright and her alert eyes peered directly at the camera, at me. I had taken that picture. That picnic occurred only one week after the miscarriage, which she had made me swear not to tell anyone about because she never wanted anyone to feel sorry for her.

I stared down at her. She'd been like a searing comet shooting through my life; now it had cooled and was an inert rock. Not having come up with a better plan, I removed a slip of paper from my pocket and began reciting the names of the diseases (most of which I couldn't pronounce)—Ulcerative Colitis, Marvan Disorder, Dysautonomia, Panic Disorder, Mantle Cell Leukemia/ Blastoid Variant—hoping that the God who Mr. Spomane encouraged me to pray to would allow Meran's soul to observe me finally accede to her desires, to acknowledge in person what had happened to her, to understand her life, to tell it straight like she had always wanted.

I doubt it'll help, but I'm going to act like it will.

Gio's Arm

While the class sat expectantly on mats in the library's basement, the licensed meditation instructor arranged a plastic lotus flower, a portrait of a Japanese monk, and charts demonstrating meditation's benefits on a folding table. There were a dozen people in the class that evening, including Quinn, and two new members scrunched together on the tattered loveseat against the concrete wall in the back—an older woman with arms wrapped maternally around a guy Quinn's age. He wore an Army t-shirt with the left sleeve hanging loose where his arm should have been. This was Guillermo.

Quinn, wearing a Lilith Fair hoodie and pink glasses with large square frames, sat with her palms on her thighs and exhaled slowly through her mouth, applying a relaxation method called "noting." The concept was to recognize emotions or thoughts, but not react to them, instead simply noting their presence without judgment.

The instructor, a spindly woman in yoga pants and hair to her waist, sat in an effortless lotus position. Her feet were bare and flecked with marks from the linoleum. A nametag in the shape of the two palms forming a mudra identified her as "Tamarra."

Quinn noted that she felt anxious but didn't judge it.

Quinn noted that she felt depressed but didn't judge it.

Quinn noted counting how much tramadol, alprazolam, and oxycodone hydrochloride remained in her pack of Newports and what sexual favors Duane would require to renew/forge more prescriptions, but didn't judge it.

"Welcome," Tamarra said, directing her attention to the two newcomers in the back, motioning them forward with her arms. "Today we are going to open with a guided meditation called Loving Kindness. This practice helps us develop compassion for ourselves and others by opening our hearts to all experience."

Quinn despised the "Loving Kindness" meditation, specifically when it prompted her to send loving kindness to someone special, someone who appreciated her the most, who held her sacred. There was no one in her life who fit that description. Last week she'd followed Tamarra to her car, a dented Jetta with a kayak in the hatchback, and asked what to do since she didn't have anyone to send loving kindness to.

Tamarra pursed her chapped lips, making a sympathetic sound.

"Remember how we said to love expansively?" Tamarra asked.

Quinn nodded, chewing on a hangnail.

"Don't fall into the trap of thinking you need a person. It can be a pet, it can be a tree or a smell, anything. The point is to generate these feelings of openness and acceptance towards self and others."

But in class that night Quinn experienced the same issues during the Loving Kindness practice. Pictures flashed through her mind and she thought of ex-boyfriends, family members, her sorority sisters, and Mr. Foltner, her psychology professor who'd sponsored her medical leave for spring semester. Nothing connected. Her intention to send loving kindness was thwarted by resentment towards these people she was supposed to love, and then she pitied herself, and soon her thoughts were no longer "with her breath" or "in the moment" but had transformed into a maelstrom of self-accusation—for what did it say about her if nobody loved or cared about her? And even though she awoke swearing not to drink that night (as usual), she then knew she would, the only question being if she'd drink alone in her mom's basement, where she had returned in failure with her dorm crates, or with strangers at Suxbees.

She opened her eyes and peeked at Guillermo, the sleeve swaying slightly from his nasal exhalations. He had sunglasses on and wore unlaced army boots. The pockets of his cargo shorts bulged.

He turned towards her.

Tamarra intoned, "Now imagine all beings, and with the full spirit of loving kindness recite the mantra silently, focused solely on how these feelings of openness and acceptance towards self and others enlarge your heart: 'May all beings be happy; may all beings be safe; may all beings be healthy; may all beings be at peace.'"

The rest of the class participants' lips moved at different paces, their backs not straight but hunched and bent, perspiration appearing at armpits and on foreheads. Some picked noses or rubbed out leg cramps. Guillermo pulled a pack of Doral Lights from a pocket and motioned with it to Quinn. When Tamarra cooed that the first session was over, and encouraged them to wiggle their fingers and toes before opening their eyes, Quinn and Guillermo were the first and only ones to leave, his mom whispering his name and asking "Donde?"

৵৹ৎড

Guillermo lit his cigarette like everyone else. Quinn had held out her lighter for him, but he just looked at her through his sunglasses and lit it with his right hand, saying, "I'm good." They were on a bench in the sculpture garden outside of the library. There were iron crescents beneath parabolic fountains, shrubs trimmed in the shapes of animals, a rock garden by the river.

"IED," Guillermo said, in a soft voice with no accent. Quinn wondered if that was something the Army did, make you lose your accent. He had a tattoo sleeve of various names and dates on his right arm.

"Improvised explosive device," said Guillermo. He and Quinn exhaled at the same time, ashing on the brick walkway beneath the "No Littering" sign.

"Those things that you drive your car and then...?" She gestured with her arms to indicate an explosion.

"A device—we can only call it a device, Army orders—detonated remotely."

The library was across from a baseball field. Following the abrupt ping of an aluminum bat, three boys ran towards home plate in succession and their teammates shouted with their hands on the railing and grins on their faces.

Guillermo pointed with his Doral towards the park's outfield fence, a plywood construction with signs advertising cable companies, pre-paid cellular data plans, credit consolidation loans.

"When I was little, this was my favorite park cuz of that fence. The other ones like in Witgen and Perksville didn't have fences, you'd just hit the ball and the kids would chase it across the street. Nobody cheered then. But here, this park, the crowd erupted. 'Cuz of the fence."

Quinn leaned over and rubbed out her butt between bricks.

Guillermo mused, "Sometimes I think that was when I hit my peak. Seven, eight years old. MVP both years. Pitched a no-hitter once, but that was before." He looked towards where his left arm would have been. With his right hand, he grabbed the hanging left sleeve and pulled it up over his shoulder, exposing the amputation site. "You can look, it's okay."

The amputation had carved out the entire shoulder, leaving a clean concavity at the arm pit, or axilla, as Guillermo explained was the anatomical term. It was hairless and custard-colored, without visible scarring. It looked like there had never been an arm there at all, as if this were just a different way for a body to be constructed. It possessed a peaceful aura, Quinn thought.

Quinn decided not to share her thoughts at the time. "I assume you don't want to hear any 'Thank You for Your Service' shit?"

Guillermo rolled his eyes.

"That why you're here?"

"..."

"Or your mom's why you're here?"

"She says I drink too much and scream in my sleep."

"Do you?"

"I'm asleep. How would I know?"

"I meant drinking."

"I drink as much as anyone else I know."

Quinn said, "I figure anything that gets me through the day is good, even if other people say it's bad, people who have no idea what's going on in my head." She pointed to her head, or rather the hoodie that covered it. "People always think it's one thing, one explanation, y'know, but everything is just…blah."

Guillermo removed a Ziploc bag filled with blue gel from his short's pocket. "VA doctors are like that too, telling me to cry, telling me to journal. They just want something to fill in their forms. I should tell them to just write blah."

There was a petri dish in the bag containing a material Quinn couldn't identify. The blue gel was a coolant, Guillermo explained, because the cellular tissue needed to remain cool to be viable for replantation.

"Replantation?"

"My arm," he elaborated, holding the bag up to the streetlights, so the tiny arm bits were illuminated. "Mo saved part of it. Off the record, the army doctors said that the tissue could be regenerated, with stem cell research."

"Why off the record?"

"It's political. VA won't cover it. And immoral, Mom says— she says this" (he gestured with his chin toward the nub) "is God challenging me and I should just accept it and move on."

"How long before you would need the procedure, like, will the tissue…expire?" Quinn winced at her diction.

Guillermo ignored the question. He lit another Doral and strolled down the sidewalk a few feet, placing the blue bag on top of a shrub trimmed in the shape of a dog. "Looks like a beret," he said, stepping back and admiring it.

"Don't play with it! Especially there—it could get poked or something." Quinn walked over, picking the bag up with both hands and holding it out to him, peering at the axilla and imagining these parts replanted into it. There would be more scarring, the peaceful aura would be erased. It was like that, life, every time you tried to fix something you ended up with something worse. Perhaps the answer was to stop thinking in terms of problems and solutions, diagnoses and prognoses, pain and cure.

Quinn observed her heart opening and recited with directed thoughts to the axilla: "May you be happy; may you be safe; may you be healthy; may you be at peace." The ballgame had ended and kids were chasing each other with water ice while their parents lingered, talking stock portfolios, housing renovations, the rear-cameras on their new SUVs.

Guillermo and Quinn just stood there, Quinn still mentally reciting the mantra, feeling for the first time that expansive love and awareness that Tamarra had promised. There was a move to be made, obvious to both, but they just stood there. Before anything could happen—it would later, after snorting pills in Suxbees' unisex bathroom—Guillermo's mom appeared outside the library door with the DOWN arrow on it and screeched, "Come! Senorita says we start. Come, Gio, we start."

Guillermo made a clucking sound with his tongue and said, with mock enthusiasm, "Indeed." He cracked his right knuckles one by one, and then tapped the bag with his arm parts five times. "When I cracked them on one hand, I always had to crack the others." He walked slowly back towards the library, the sloping lane making him appear to grow smaller as he receded.

"Hey!" Quinn called after him, still holding the bag. "What about this?"

"There's no hurry."

Where We Marched, His Final Years

Here's a picture of Dad and me marching at the Inauguration Protest, January 20th, 2017, him holding the IMPEACH TRUMP sign I duct-taped to his hand. He voted for Trump but that didn't matter—what mattered, according to his neurologist, was that he get fresh air, sunlight, and exercise, away from the confinements of Lush Horizons. This picture, yes, that's him marching with the pink Breast Cancer Awareness cap at the Women's March, January 21st. His gait palsied, hands slapping the air, mind still in the sixties, the decade he said ruined America, the decade I was born.

At the airport, on January 28th, we marched against the Trump Travel Ban.

In Lassing Park, on April 29th, we marched for People's Climate Change.

During the marches, he had lucid moments when he'd suddenly look around at the spectacle of half-clothed college students taking Instas and Snaps, middle-aged women screaming into megaphones like rock stars, the squeal of vuvuzelas. He'd croak my name like he didn't know I was there, but I'd just push him on, saying "Everything's okay, Pop."

Was it wrong of me to do this? Maybe it was because every time I watched the news I thought of him, with a sort of "double consciousness," always arguing against him in my head.

"You love him too much," my therapist said.

"I can't stop thinking of him," I said.

She folded her hands. "Love can be very frustrating."

Is my account of Alzheimer's just literary, a figuration, a synecdoche for media saturation? When Obama was elected, Dad, still lucid, entered a different world. FOX News. Drudge Report. Breitbart. Limbaugh. Our weekly dinners devolved into polite discussions about the weather and traffic, tending to Mom's grave, and was I dating any special women. I was fifty-two, he was seventy-five. We'd drink two Michelob Ultras, then shake hands.

We joined the National Pride March, June 11th.

We joined March for Black Women, September 20th.

We joined March for Our Lives, March 24, 2018, three weeks before I removed him from the ventilation machine.

After March for Our Lives, I put him to bed in Lush Horizons, changing his diaper and applying lotion to his lower joints. He was exhausted, but made a clicking sign that meant turn on the TV. FOX was running a story about Hillary's servers. Dad sighed. I remembered that sigh from childhood, when I'd appear at the dinner table with black nails, claim Reagan was a war criminal at family parties, or refuse to attend church.

I got into bed with him and secured the bed rails. "I love you too much, is the problem," I whispered.

He motioned me closer, his face grimacing, and pointed at the TV. "Lock her up."

"Yeah," I said, placing another pillow under his withered head. Then I rested my cheek against his heart, like when I was a kid and had nightmares. "Lock her up, Pop."

Holy Aurations

Evan Klankerty avoided The Dancin' Bare for eight days after he stuck his business card into Caelin's thong. Since the stomach pains had started two months ago, just before his fortieth birthday, his frequency in visiting the club had increased from weekly to daily, and his attraction to Caelin developed from something purely sexual to what he now considered love. He declined to be serviced by any of the other dancers, patiently sitting in the corner by the Trivia! machine, where he'd record inspiring quotes in what his therapist called his "Positivity Journal" until Caelin appeared on stage, lit by compact fluorescents, aiming a smile at him as she scanned the men in the club, her dreamcatcher belly-chain coiling around the stripper's pole.

On that last night, he copied on the back of his business card: *A thing of beauty is a joy forever—Keats.* Caelin and he were in the back room, which used LED "spot lighting" to illuminate the dancers but leave the customers feeling unexposed. After slipping the card with a wad of twenties into Caelin's thong, he asked her what the dreamcatcher chain signified.

Caelin swayed with her hands behind her head, eyes closed, less than a foot from him. She notched his knees apart and moved in closer. "It's just something to help when I'm in trouble."

"Are you in trouble?"

"Do I look like I am?" she asked, smiling luridly. She grinded harder into him and grabbed his shoulders, a nipple he wasn't permitted to touch grazing his double chin, her red hair tickling his receding hairline, and they didn't talk anymore that night.

The business card identified him as a substance abuse counselor at Keystone Services, Lancaster, PA, and included his office and cell phone numbers, his office and private email addresses, and at the bottom a John Lennon quote: *While There's Life There's Hope.* In the days after he'd given Caelin his card, Evan had lived in a state of fluctuating hope. Every time the phone rang or his email chirped, he imagined it was Caelin and told himself a story about being her boyfriend, sharing his life with her. Sometimes he let the phone sit with the call missed or the email unopened, increasing the zone of expectation to hours during which he would tell himself even more elaborate stories about his future with Caelin. Eventually, though, he would check the phone message or email in a state of exhilaration and instantly become depressed and hopeless, again, because the only people who called or emailed him were credit collectors, telemarketers, or colleagues asking him to cover their shifts.

ஐ௸

That Tuesday evening was one dollar domestics and unlimited wings for five bucks at The Dancin' Bare, but Evan, who'd agreed to cover a colleague's overnight shift, was in the Keystone office writing progress notes and counting medications.

Evan worried that his phone had stopped working. Its last activity had occurred four days ago, a computer-generated reminder of his procedure at the clinic tomorrow morning. Cell phones, like the rest of the changes that had erupted since his childhood, made Evan feel lonely. The whole world made him feel lonely, like it wasn't the world he had been prepared for as a child. There should be support groups for people his age, he mused, not the infirm or demented but those too old to understand things like Tinder, Zelle, FWB, 24/7 news cycles, the continuous flow of possibilities within grasp for everyone but him. He winced, telling himself that the stomach pain was just an ulcer or something and not cancer, as Dr. Chen said was just a possibility they needed to rule out.

Evan's phone vibrated, revealing a local number, then beeped, indicating a voice message. Evan pocketed his phone and went out onto the front porch of the building. He eased himself onto the porch's stained loveseat and pressed the voicemail button. For what felt like a whole minute there was static, but then within that static, within that noise, he finally detected a signal. A female voice, cracking.

"Evan?" the voice sniffled, "I'm in trouble." There was a muffled sound. The phone clattered and the voice returned, speaking faster. "It's Caelin, please come. I don't know. It's just—nevermind." The connection cut.

Evan called and left a message asking for the address when there was no answer. He paced the perimeter of the facility, imagining finally kissing her, touching her hair, all those intimate maneuvers forbidden by the club. There were still a few residents in the lobby, pale and gaunt in the TV's sedative light, but every other room was dark. He forwarded the office phone to his cell and got in the facility's van.

ఌ౮

His phone lit up with a text message from Caelin's number, providing her address, warning him to turn the headlights off by the barn so her parents wouldn't see. He was surprised, arriving at her parents' property, to see that it functioned as a real dairy farm, with the smells and sounds he associated with them from the Amish on TV. An image of her as a young girl in a purple dress riding a bicycle appeared in his mind, reminding him of one of the core Substance Abuse mantras: You can never tell where people are from, or where they are going.

The moon here, away from the city, was engorged and lit up the acres. He panted, leaning down into the shadows of the farm's brooding structures, breathing deeply when he got to the basement door. He saw lit candles inside between the curtains. The candles surrounded an air-mattress on the floor where Caelin sat Indian-style. There were myriad ripped and sad-looking stuffed animals, some held together with safety pins, some missing eyes, limbs. The dreamcatcher chain hung over her on the wall, like a crucifix in some story about vampires, as perhaps this story is. Her shoulders were hunched and her head was bowed. There were clothes strewn about the floor and a futon and supplies—Ziploc bag, razor, grayish crumbs—on a chicken crate next to the air mattress. He tapped on the glass.

"I shouldn't have asked you to come," she slurred, sliding the door open with both arms. He tried to inspect the supplies by her mattress without being too obvious, realizing fatalistically that she wasn't sober enough to consent to intimate activity.

"I always let people down," she sniffled. She was wearing sweatpants, a black hoodie dotted with cat fur, and wool winter socks. "I'm broken."

"Don't say that," Evan said, smiling broadly. "I'm glad that you called; everyone has bad nights." She pulled her hoodie down, strands of hair cascading out, greasy and thin. She looked in his direction but didn't make eye contact. There were acne marks on her face. Her eyes were red, pupils dilated, nostrils abraded. The rest of her face was pale, the piercings removed, her lips chapped. There was something about her now, with her acne and sweats, which was more attractive and...substantial, he thought, than the exotic dancing figure he had thought he'd known before.

"I wouldn't have called if I knew I'd bump," she said.

"That's normal," Evan said. "Be proud that you tried. It's almost impossible to do alone, you know," he said, easing himself onto the futon.

"I thought I could." She shrugged again, like it was all she could do. "It's like I do it against my will. I love it more than, more than...everything. I love it more than *me*, but I mean who would I even be without it?" She lit a cigarette, resting it on top of a Diet Coke can with ashes around its mouth.

"Caelin." Evan crouched towards her. He realized that tonight was about her, not him; he hoped he could help her without any distractions, to be mindful of her fragility. "These are all normal symptoms. I can help. I mean, did you call me because you saw where I worked?"

"Jill."

"What?"

"My name. Caelin's for the stage." She smeared her hand against her nose and stood, walking across the room holding the can and flicking ash into it. She looked so small and endearingly plain without her heels.

He shifted on the futon and grimaced, holding his stomach, which was starting to cramp. He inhaled deeply and exhaled slowly.

"You okay?" she asked.

"Just this—" he motioned to his left side.

"What is it?"

"Cancer?" He chuckled. "I'm trying to look on the bright side."

She turned on a lamp, crouching beside the futon and palpating his side gently. "Here?" she asked, kneading with bony fingers. "Here?"

"Around there."

"Take your shirt off," she said.

Evan removed his jacket and pulled his shirt over his head. "Now I feel like a stripper," he joked, embarrassed about his expanding paunch.

Jill took a nursing textbook from the end table and told him to stand up. She was suddenly sharp and lucid, he noticed, a common tendency for addicts when given a task to focus on. She felt his torso in four quadrants, checking the textbook, asking him to scale the pain from 1-10. When she was done, she asked if there were other physical symptoms, such as digestive, excretory, or bladder changes.

"No," he lied.

"Have you seen someone?"

"I'm supposed to in the morning."

"Supposed to?"

Evan put his shirt back on and sat down, his elbows on his knees. "It's nothing, I'm not going."

Jill looked at him, maybe for the first time ever, after all the simulations at The Dancin' Bare, with actual care in her eyes. "You need to do this."

"You need to go to rehab. That's serious, too."

"This takes an hour. Rehab is for life." She lit another cigarette. "Tell me you'll go."

"I don't have a ride anyway," he said. He honestly didn't know whether he said this in order to suggest she drive him.

They paused in silence, looking at one another. As usual, he was sitting and she was standing, in a position of power, pondering him as though she were thousands of miles away.

"What time is the appointment?" she asked.

"Seven-thirty."

She focused on the wavering tip of the cigarette as she missed flicking the ash into the can's mouth. "I want to see the sunrise, to feel it on my skin. I'm a fucking vampire, this life." She dropped the cigarette into the can with a *pzzz* sound and slipped on a pair of ratty Chuck Taylors, gently pulling him to his feet. "So, I'm taking you. I'll see my sunrise and you'll get a clean bill of health. What would I do without you?"

෨൙

Jill drove the van in a seeming reverie, swerving onto the back roads leading to the quarry. She braked and turned the engine off, hunching, silent and motionless, watching the sun's ray's angle over cracked rocks and water holes. It was so quiet in the van he could hear her breathing, *tachycardia*, her blood not oxygenating. Evan remembered coming here as a teenager, getting high and leaping into the water, or later sitting in his dad's idling Oldsmobile with girls from Penn State Main, passing a flask of whiskey back and forth, listening to the Allman Brothers bootlegs and talking about their futures.

He told her about these memories but she didn't respond, instead resting her chin on the steering wheel, like a child peering at something unattainable. She closed her eyes, whispered something to herself, and then reversed the car back to the main road and drove to the clinic's empty parking lot.

"Party time!" she said, turning the engine off.

After Evan signed in at the front desk, they sat on wooden chairs, the only people in the waiting room filled with fake plants, canned laughter from TV game shows, and magazines splayed on the tables between chairs. Evan stared at *Cancer Today* and muttered to Jill, "They could at least pretend I'm not dying."

"I need to use the bathroom." Jill stood up and took the dreamcatcher chain from her pocket. "Take this with you, if I'm not back—"

"Why wouldn't you be back?"

"Just take it." She pulled his fingers open and unspooled the dreamcatcher chain into his palm. "Make sure they hang it somewhere you can see it. Look at it and think positive thoughts."

She rushed into the bathroom, locking the door. He followed her and heard snorting sounds and she didn't respond to him asking her to unlock the door, banging gently so as not to alert the receptionists.

Then a nurse called him into the pre-op room, where people removed his clothing and offered him a smock. The nurse hung the dreamcatcher on one of those human anatomy charts where he fixed his eyes on it while Dr. Chen explained the operation's objectives to him. Meanwhile a tall man in white injected him with something and he counted backwards from a hundred. He didn't fall asleep, but he didn't dream either. It was more like entering an alternate reality that was just as real as the previous one. He imagined Jill operating on him, scoping and scanning not his stomach, but rather his heart. She spoke into a microphone, intoning "The results of the procedure to determine whether Evan Klankerty is a good person were inconclusive." As he came out of the anesthesia, he thought he saw a quote from his Positivity

Journal on the wall where the anatomy chart had been. It was Thoreau: *Could a greater miracle take place than for us to look through each other's eyes for an instant?*

Jill was gone when he came out of the operating room. He never forgot about her, remembering her not as she was on the pole but as she was in her basement that winter night, with her hoodie and acne and Chucks, her used nursing textbook, her look of despair at the quarry. He slept with Jill's dreamcatcher chain wrapped around his Positivity Journal on the bedside table. Sometimes he would think about texting her, asking her if she was okay, if she needed someone to talk to, but he knew it was wrong.

By then, Evan Klankerty was taking it one day at a time, spending his evenings not in clubs but strolling around the neighborhood, smelling manure and cut grass, watching kids throwing footballs or playing tag, or else he was tanning in his front yard, unconcerned about what people would say about his body's appearance. It was fifteen months later—a full year beyond his initial prognosis—that he saw her picture in the obituary section of the paper, Jill Rosen, twenty-three. There was no cause of death provided. He mailed Jill's dreamcatcher chain to the listed memorial home, along with a brief note explaining how she had saved his life.

When he finally expired—Girl Scouts coming to the door reported seeing his body through the window—the service was attended by freelancer grievers hired by the funeral home and a few tranquilized Keystone residents. Since nobody knew him well enough to speak, the funeral home's director simply read some selected quotes from Evan's Positivity Journal. He'd had his assistant make some laminated bookmarks at Kinkos for twenty dollars, consisting of one quote along with Evan's picture from his Keystone security badge. The quote was from "Imagine," about not being the only one who was a dreamer.

The attendees left their bookmarks on the floor or on their seats when the memorial was over and, as he cleaned up, tossing them in a CVS bag they used as trash can liners, the director tried to imagine who Evan Klankerty really was, on the inside, aurated in holy singularity. He recalled his own father's injunction that their work's mission was to reveal that even the most seemingly empty life was ablaze with exceptional hopes and acts of kindness, and dreams that, for all we know, he thought, locking the memorial's newly painted doors, have already come true in other worlds, or universes, or whatever people wished to call them according to their own personal cosmologies or belief systems.

Theory of Mind

What follows is the story of how I became a Lying Machine, and then, because of *Mind-Reading,* Maddy's memoir, became human again. It started with a Craigslist advertisement for a "Virtual Reviewer" from a company called Millennial Media. I'd been out of college for over six months and had yet to receive a callback from an interview. I was living with Mom after Maddy kicked me out after hearing about Valerie Canessa, or crashing on friends' couches. Maddy was staying at our old apartment alone, my boxes of books and video games in the guest room's closet along with Ernie's toys. Ernie was still in the institute, recovering from the incident with their father.

The interview at Millennial Media was conducted by Dr. Dulminer, a slim woman whose steel face betrayed no emotion.

"This interview has only one question," she stated, "with a few subordinate follow-ups." She motioned to me to sit down without looking at me. "Not 'Do you lie?'" she said, "because everyone does, but 'Do you believe your lies?'"

"Is that a trick question?" I asked. "Like if I tell the truth I'm lying?"

"Just answer the question, Kenny," Dr. Dulminer sighed. "This isn't philosophy class."

I thought about the question. I'd certainly lied before, but I always thought they were merited lies, or what Mom called "God's white lies." There were times, though, I remembered, like with Maddy, that I actually believed in the lies the more she didn't, like *in the moment* I believed myself sincere in saying

I hadn't fucked Valerie Canessa at Maxton's bachelor party. I thought of the terrible stories I had written at Penn State, thinly fictionalized exploits of my sex life, Dad's cancer, war stories based on movies from the seventies. In my creative writing class, we'd discussed Hemingway's dictum that fiction can be truer than fact, if told right.

"I don't see a difference between fiction and non-fiction," I started, preparing to elaborate upon Hemingway's theory and things that Maddy, whose major was Cognitive Psychology, had told me about how narratives, whether fictive or non-fictive, affected our social skills and understanding of others. She said this was based on something called Theory of Mind, which was a little like mind-reading, and it was because of a deficit of Theory of Mind that Ernie was so far to the left on the spectrum.

"So, you believe your lies, yes?" Dr. Dulminer checked off something on her e-tablet. "And would you say then also that other people believe your lies, that you're a good liar?"

"It's not something I'm proud of, but yeah, sure," I said, motioning with my hand like it was obvious.

She nodded. "Everybody thinks that. And then," Dr. Dulminer said, making more notes on her e-tablet with a stylus, "how do you feel about lies, in terms of things like morals or ethics?" She made air quotes with her fingers when saying 'morals' and 'ethics.'

I didn't understand what she meant at first, so I just said what came to my mind. "I think mainly when I lie, I'm trying to figure out if the person believes me or not. Usually I end up thinking that if it's so easy for me to lie to people they're probably lying to me, too." I shrugged.

"So, no guilt?"

"No," I said.

"And you consider yourself a good one?"

"I get the feeling that you think I am," I stated.

"We think you could be." She pulled my resume from a binder and placed it on the table between us. Clearing aside various trade magazines—*Brain and Language, Cognitive Psychology, Journal of Interactive Marketing*—she pointed to items on my resume. "Like this here, where you write that you were editor of a student magazine and oversaw all aspects of design, submissions, advertising, and so forth. This is what we call a *plausible lie*." She pointed with her tapered finger, like a sword. "Nobody believes you did all those things, but then nobody doubts it enough to investigate. The essence of this job will be to use your writing ability to compose plausible lies: lies that you believe, lies that humans believe, lies that bypass computer algorithms. Reviews, to be technical, not lies."

"Reviews of what?"

"You've heard of the Turing Test," she said, as she powered off her tablet and returned my resume to her binder. I couldn't tell if it was a statement or a question. "The test is about what we recognize as human and computer," she said. "Follow me. We'll see what Turing thinks."

We walked through modular halls, fluorescently lit, the walls curving into and out of open atrial lounges, vast spaces where workers sat before terminals with headphones, dressed in everything from jeans to work-out gear to pajamas. An older man with an unbuttoned paisley shirt and sandals stalked along a treadmill as he dictated into a CPU slotted into the unit's head module. There were muscle balls and climbing walls, and a Kiddie Funhouse with Ping-Pong tables and rows of Wii Consoles, and above it a sign that read "Express Yourself!"

"These are the reviewers," Dr. Dulminer said, motioning to the young professionals. "They call themselves Lying Machines, not Sockpuppets, not Yahooboys, they hate that. This is where you'll start."

Then she stopped and waved me into a room the size of a prison cell or large bathroom, empty except for a laptop on a table and a chair. She gave me a business card with login credentials for the computer.

"Let's get started," she said. "Take some time to look around the various sites bookmarked under the Review Test folder," she directed me. I saw Yelp, Amazon, Google Local, Goodreads, and a number of other social media and local review sites.

"These are test reviews," she said. "They're meant to decipher how persuasive and plausibly you can lie. For the Yelp product, give it a 1-star rating and explain in the review what was so bad about it; for the Amazon product, give it a 3-star rating and explain what was so average about it; for Google Local business, give it a 5-star rating and explain what was so great about it. Write uniquely, in detail, not too positive or negative. You need to avoid detection by the site algorithms, that's where Turing comes in. Use your creative writing training—lie, tell stories, narrate, come up with something so believable you yourself think it's true. We will evaluate these to see if you are a Pro or Con."

"Pro or Con?"

"That means are you better at lying and saying things are good, or lying and saying things are bad."

"Which is better?"

"Wave when you're done," she said, pointing at the camera mounted in the corner of the room. "I'll be watching."

ଽଏଓଷ

It turned out I was a Con. I was stationed in a cubicle next to Klova, a square-shaped woman in her early thirties who was also a Con. She wore square red-and-black mirrored glasses that reminded me of Terminator's eye. We became friendly, laughing over smoothies and wraps at lunch about the negative reviews we had composed during the day. She'd also graduated with an MFA in English, and showed me how to not just write reviews, but how to embed reviews into stories and larger, more humanistic, narratives. "If you think about it," she explained, the two of us walking on treadmills at the office gym, "a typical story, a literary story, is a *review* of the world, or of your life. So, these reviews, whatever they are regarding, can be as literary and stimulating as the best stories."

As proof of this, she showed me reviews she had gotten published as microfictions in *McSweeneys* under the pseudonym

Minda Harraway. She continued: "What sucks about most jobs is the reality of them. They lock your brain into one task and say 'repeat.' Which kills people. Literally. Especially creatives like us. But in this job, Kenny, in this job we invent something new every day, and since we're Cons we can be negative and never get shit for it, like in the real world. People don't like when you tell the truth, that's why I like it here." It didn't take me long to understand what she meant.

Maddy had always said that I was too negative, that I saw the worst in everything, leading to her nicknaming me "Half Empty." "Coming from where I did, I had to fight for everything, nobody was on my side, nobody helped, it's always been a struggle, but I don't complain because I know there are people who've had it far worse," she'd told me once. "You though, you're so smart, you have a great mom, your health, your scholarships, and it's like everything's a bother for you, nothing is good enough."

After six months, the company officially hired me, assigning me to work on a campaign for Dyskordia Press. The campaign's Con agenda was to locate competitors' book releases on sites such as Barnes and Noble, Amazon, Goodreads, and Powell's, and write reviews about how bad they were, whereas the Pro agenda was to perform the opposite for books releases by Dyskordia Press. I began to write elaborate reviews about how bad Dyskordia's competitors' books were, which I enjoyed because I was twenty-five and still hadn't had a story published myself, and was frustrated because everything I saw that was published and winning awards and receiving acclaim sucked (or so I thought). Being a Lying Machine helped me express my resentment at constant rejection, which I suppose was therapeutic. However, being paid to be negative turned out to have certain unintended consequences, one of which was that I became even *more* negative and disconnected than before.

My mom informed me, her arms folded, that I could cook my own meals from now on because I was too critical of her cooking. The friends I had been staying with said they didn't want me around their kids because of my foul language and bitter attitude. Worst of all, Maddy, whom I had started talking to again, stopped responding, saying she needed to focus on positive things for both herself and Ernie.

"I told you, you need to change," she had said over the phone. I was in my bedroom at Mom's house, constantly changing the TV channels because nothing good was on. "I'm sorry to say that, like I think I'm *all that*. Believe me, Kenny, I know I'm nothing special, and I don't want it to sound like an ultimatum, but I can only let you into my life again if I can trust you and you work on your attitude. You keep saying you've changed and I want to believe it because I love you, but then you always go back to same old Half-Empty Kenny."

I sighed. "Look, I'm not being negative here, I'm just saying that I wouldn't be negative if you'd take me back, like it's not fair for you to demand I change without allowing for the circumstances of my life to change, which would affect my attitude, obviously. I can only prove things have changed if you take me back, live with you, spend time with you and Ernie. Not just texting or talking once in a while, like, how could that work? It's a relationship, there are two people involved, right?"

"I don't think I can."

Ultimately, I didn't have particularly intense feelings about any of these developments, even about Maddy, because lying for a living, especially in a negative way, affected my own Theory of Mind, my ability to actually connect with other human beings. This was my mentality when I arrived at work one rainy Thursday in summer and sat down to write a review of the memoir *Mind-Reading*, published by Andora Press, a division of one of the big publishing houses, authored by my ex-girlfriend, Madeline Haddstra.

Normally, we didn't actually *read* the books we reviewed. At least the Cons—I think the Pros tended to, because longer reviews correlated with positive emotion. It was normally enough for us Cons to read the beginning and end, skim the middle, check out some other reviews and whatever we could find online, and then construct our reviews from there, the same way I had pretended to read boring books when I was in college.

"Check this out," Klova said. She wore her cyborg sunglasses and had her bare feet with black toenails up on her desk, her keyboard balanced on her lap. We'd been spending more and more time together, talking about how stupid and inferior other people were—that and our ambitions as writers were our only commonalities. I'd started sleeping over at her place to avoid my mom, but only on her couch, because she said she was scared to sleep next to someone; she thought they would stab her in her sleep. Nothing romantic was happening between us; she had a sort of asexual vibe.

"There's this cheesy memoir about autism," she said, "so I'm reviewing it as an autistic person. Pretending to be on the autism spectrum, whatever. It's really an effective writing exercise. We should have done it for the MFA, like pretend you have a disability and write like Artaud or Helen Keller. Except how would the teacher grade that, I guess?"

She flash-mapped her file onto my monitor and said, "I'm going to play that new video game, the one where you can be anyone in history. I want to be Gertrude Stein." I watched her limp (she had a screw in her knee from a skateboarding accident) down the long rows of Lying Machines, all laughing and typing, J.T. and Marcus playing Ping-Pong, the Plasma TVs on the walls showing cartoons, sports shows, reality shows. I spun back around and read what Klova had written:

> this story mind-reading says it is about autism but it is not about autism what the human being says makes no sense to me especially when the human being talks about her brother her brother has autism too the human being says i do not understand him or the human being why would the human being publish a book about autism if the human being does not understand autism I am glad I am not the human being's brother do not waste your time or money i wish i had more money to buy video games with do you have some money

I thought then of Ernie. He wasn't one of those people with autism you see in movies or documentaries, like *Rainman* or Temple Grandin or those adolescent chess grandmasters. He was in no way an *idiot savant* or gifted. He was just a lonely kid, taking apart his Transformers and putting them back together. He used to bang his head against the wall, wailing "It's Not, It's Not" until someone restrained him.

That was a long time ago, when I first met Ernie. Maddy and I had begun dating during junior year and she'd taken me home for fall break to meet her dad and Ernie, who was eight then. She'd warned me that Ernie was protective of her, especially from men, and capable of extreme violence, or "Retard Strength" as my less enlightened friends called it. My intention had been to leave in the morning and return to campus to spend the weekend with Valerie Canessa. Although I didn't consider my relationship with Maddy as anything special, I knew that being nice to her brother would help get me in her pants, and during all the activities I'd shared with him that day (as I remembered now, sitting in my Lying Machine cubicle), I'd been thinking of precisely that, fucking her for the first time.

Her house was like something from a horror movie. It was at the end of a deserted lane, its paint chipped, planks stacked on the sagging front porch, dismantled cars around the dying yellow lawn that featured no toys, no bicycles or footballs or jump ropes. I'd expected to see them, considering that a little boy lived there.

"Thank God," said, Maddy, parking in front of a huge plastic container overflowing with compacted Budweiser cans.

"What?" I asked. The door of her 2001 Volvo screeched as I got out.

"My dad's not here."

"Good," I said. I wasn't looking forward to meeting her dad, especially after she'd described him as a temperamental alcoholic with violent tendencies.

"Let me go inside first to see Ernie," Maddy said. "I want to prepare him." We hugged in front of the car. "Stop worrying, Kenny, I just want my little man to myself for a second."

When Maddy finally came back out and opened the front door with its ripped screen, she was holding a skinny boy with tiny wrists and hair cut in tufts. His spindly legs dangled and his body was half turned, hugging her, avoiding eye contact with me. He wore a faded NASCAR t-shirt and brown wrinkled slacks that were too big for him, almost covering the Velcro straps on his sneakers.

"Come in!" Maddy said. I remember her wearing one of those vintage dresses she had. She looked so maternal holding Ernie. "Ernie can't wait to meet you."

At first he wouldn't make eye-contact or respond to my comments or jokes, but when we were playing Monopoly we both wanted to be the thimble and, after some encouragement from Maddy about the virtues of sharing, he put the thimble in my palm and I clasped it, our hands holding together. I made a monster sound before giving the thimble back to him, and he sort of giggled.

We sat cross-legged on the floor in the living room. After we let Ernie win at Monopoly, he wanted us to play with his Legos. When he stumbled down the hall to get them, Maddy stretched and said, "I'm going to take a shower and make dinner."

"Is he cool alone with me? What if your dad comes?"

She cradled my head with her hands and kissed me in a vertical progression: forehead, nose, lips. "He likes you, Kenny. You'll be fine."

Ernie and I played with his Legos and he showed me his favorite video games. I overheard Maddy arguing on the phone with her dad and dinner kept getting pushed back. Ernie and I were snacking on Goldfish crackers and watching an old episode of *Inspector Gadget* when Maddy, wearing an apron, announced that dinner was finally ready.

"Without him?" Ernie asked.

"He'll be late buddy. It'll just be us three."

"Can we eat out here?" he asked, excited.

She skipped into the room and tousled his hair. "Anything you want, little man."

I was doing the dishes when headlights appeared in the yard and a pickup lurched to a stop right behind Maddy's Volvo, blocking her in. She was in the bathroom with Ernie, fixing his hair. It was about ten o'clock. I turned off the faucet and moved away from the sink, drying my hands on my jeans, when her dad lumbered through the door, drinking a beer and holding the remaining five of the six-pack in his right hand with his keys. He raised the dangling beers and asked, "Brewski?"

The last time I'd had a Budweiser was when my dad let me sip from his while watching Phillies games, before his cancer.

He tossed one to me, finished his, crinkled it in his massive hands, and opened another. "You Ken?"

"It's nice to meet you, sir."

"Of course it is," he joked. "I'm king of the county." He drank half the beer and looked around the kitchen.

"There's spaghetti in the fridge. We waited but Ernie was hungry."

"She always over boils spaghetti. I mean Ken, who can't boil spaghetti? Just between us." He walked closer to me and I could smell strong liquor on his breath. "Her mother couldn't either, I don't know how to pick 'em, I tell you Ken. Where is she?" He started to shout her name, "Mad!" and lurched out of the kitchen.

That night ended with Maddy's dad berating her in front of Ernie for the B grade she'd gotten in Advanced Calculus. "I bet even Ernie here could get better then a B, right Ernie?"

We were all in the living room together, her dad finishing off his six-pack. Maddy had just given Ernie a bath and he sat in her lap while she combed his hair. He looked like the happiest boy in the world.

"Ernie?" her dad knocked on his own head with the empty can. "You understand anything? I asked you a question."

"Dad," Maddy said, "just stop. He's never even heard of calculus."

"According to this," he flicked the registrar's Grade Report, "neither have you."

Maddy sighed. "I did the best I could," she said. "I'm happy with it."

"I'm not, I'm not happy about it at all. It was bad enough with one retard, now I have two."

"Don't use that word."

"I'll use whatever words I want in my house." He crushed the can on a side table strewn with *Hustler* and NASCAR magazines and ripped Ernie from Maddy's hands. "Bed time, bub."

Ernie reached back for Maddy, but his dad threw him over his shoulder and staggered down the hallway, telling at him to grow up and act like a man, Ernie screeching *"Ken Stay, Ken Stay."*

Maddy and I spent that night on the floor in Ernie's room, watching him sleep. He had some metal thing strapped into his jaw to prevent his teeth from grinding. At one point she started removing my jeans and bent her head down but I whispered, "We don't have to, let's just hold each other."

"I really want to."

"With him in here?" I kissed her. "Believe me I want this more than you can imagine, I guess you can tell that," I laughed, and she did too.

"Kenny?"

"I'm here."

"I really like you," she said. "You're not like the others." She kissed me and tucked her head under my chin. "I love watching him sleep, it's like I know he's okay then at least." Maddy fell asleep before me. I remembered that I stayed up most of the night looking at the two of them, comparing their sleeping faces, looking around the room with its chipped wall paint, dusty furniture, the bed shaped like a race car.

I wondered whether Ernie was still in the institution he'd been placed in after his father held Ernie's face in the toilet. I pictured Maddy alone in the apartment, looking through photo albums or writing in her diary with the pink clouds. Despite her brother's disabilities, her mother's death, her father's alcoholism, she was the most optimistic person I knew.

The cover of *Mind-Reading* was almost an exact copy of my memory's image of Maddy standing in that dank house's doorway, wearing a dress, holding Ernie in front of her. Even though I could have acquired it for free by looting the Dyskordia Press slush pile, I purchased it and mailed it to our apartment with a note saying, "Check my Amazon review." Klova was saying something in that snarky voice of hers but I wasn't paying attention; I was done with people like her. I began to write a review of the book based on my recollections of Maddy and Eddie as individuals, and the three of us as a family. I wrote it under my own name, not as a Sockpuppet. At the end of the review, I wrote, "This memoir reminds the reader to always view the glass as half-full " and hit SUBMIT.

Red Tide

The red tide appeared her first night at Arcadia Shores, cloaked in darkness, a sinister presence on Florida's Atlantic coast. It was the summer of 2018.

Chemicals had brought both the red tide and Serena to Florida. The red tide denotes a variety of algal blooms, such as *k. brevis.*, fed by agricultural runoff and lawn fertilizers, which discolor water, kill marine life, and depress the Florida tourist industry. For Serena, the chemicals were oxy, bennies, and gabapentin. It was only after her third overdose had been uploaded to YouTube that she'd been convinced to enter rehab.

Serena and Tara, the newbies, slouched by the rehab's pool at one of those tables with a looming umbrella, watching overdose videos on YouTube:

"Dead at Walgreens Heroin OVERDOSE."

"Father Videoing His Daughter's Overdose."

"Teens Film Parents Who Overdosed on Heroin."

The rest of the people at the pool were from the motel—the rehab and the motel, two halves of a former apartment complex, shared a pool in what was an imperfect arrangement at best. I could always tell the motel-people from the rehab-people simply based on who was drinking and their general demeanor: ebullience versus apathy. For example, in the deep end of the pool there were a bunch of college-aged kids, bronzed and toned, the girls whooping on the guys' shoulders, holding aloft beers in insulated Koozies. This was in opposition to Serena, my Serena, the only one there in long sleeves, and Tara. They were getting used to being No Fun. Heads were slumped on wrists as they looked at the tablet they'd checked out for the night.

"They blackmail people with them," Tara said, pointing at the video of two parents seizing on kitchen tiles. She had leathery skin and tattoos everywhere.

Serena glanced over at the beach, where people had gathered.

"My friend said totally," Tara added. "It happened to someone she knew."

The website had described Arcadia Shores as "a coastal Florida refuge," but the coast was no longer safe, what with dead fish washing up through the tide in stacked piles, and scavenger birds limping around, stumbling, intoxicated. A marine biologist at the Recovery Group Meeting yesterday had said the birds were drinking flushed opiates from the marshes and bayous. The birds. She joked that the birds would join them here in recovery soon. I'd watched it on the scanner rerun-feed.

Another way of telling that Serena and Tara were from Arcadia Shores was the red biometric bracelets they wore on their wrists and ankles. These transmitted vital signs, GPS, and chemistry to our lab in the "Nerd Cave," which used to be the apartment complex's indoor racquetball court. We used this information to quantify data and develop advanced statistical models for recovery/relapse. The lab/Nerd Cave smelled like chronic and was full of bookish, immature guys crouched over laptops, like a dorm. Serena was my first client, although she didn't know it. In fact, none of them knew that we existed, technically.

The activity on the beach had increased. There were loud shouts and speedboats motoring towards shore. The college kids popped out of the pool and wrapped towels around themselves, pointing at the bonfire on the beach, its smoke sine-waving over the pool.

They skipped over to Serena and Tara. One of the girls asked, holding her nose, "Is that the red tide?"

Tara nodded.

"What are they doing?"

"Burning."

A guy with long blonde hair and tattoos of wings on his feet explained, "Burning reduces the smell, Lizzy."

"They're burning corpses, dude." Serena muttered.

They all looked at Serena. She was wearing black leggings and an *It's Always Sunny in Philadelphia* t-shirt.

"Can we do it, too?"

"You want to burn?" Serena had already developed a reputation as The Bitch from Philly.

"Let's go," Tara said. "They don't care; I do it all the time."

After the others had scrambled away, Serena watched her own personal overdose video. It showed her with her niece in a grocery store. Serena was on the ground, twitching, glasses broken and knuckles chafed against the linoleum. Tendrils of blood washed up against the Tide detergent, diffusing into bread wraps, produce bags, diapers. Little Mable in her Miss Piggy parka was seen crying, "Seren! Seren! Seren!" until a policewoman took her away and the video cut.

She watched it on a loop and then closed the tab when Tara and the others returned, wet and panting, eyes red. They said how sad it was. "I will never forget that image," one said; "I didn't pay for this," said another. They brought out vapes and THC gummies and handed them around. The tall guy looked at them and smirked, "I guess you two can't, huh?"

"I can!" exclaimed Tara. Back in the Nerd Lab, Stevie put down his cell phone and brought up her account on his laptop, updating her progress notes with various input codes for deviance.

Serena stumbled away through the sand with the tablet, towards the bonfire. Guitars played to a dancing jubilance around the dead heap of marine life. There was a pungent necrotic smell. She pulled up her video and again, for maybe the hundredth time since last month, scoured the video's comments, most of which posited opinions along the lines of "She's a loser" and "She deserves to die!" But among these was were some from my anon Google handle writing: "I know her!" "Please pray for her!" "She is a good woman!" And neither for the first time nor the last, she copied my handle's email address and wrote "Who are you?"— never guessing I was only one hundred yards away, my phone's push notification vibrating, following her on video, my muse, my *raison d'etre*, knowing I wouldn't let this one get away.

Ambushing the Void II

The project manager, Epistell, gestured toward the projector
screen and said, "What I've asked you here to discuss may seem
morbid, but it will be the centerpiece of the newspaper industry
in this new digital economy." He then distributed the Revised
Obituary Templates (Form 33–34, Rev_3). The forms were
divided into five sections: Narration, Illustration, Exposition,
Memoration, and Singulation—what he would later call the
NIEMS Method. There were seven of us freelancers in the 25th-
floor conference room, wearing borrowed suits, taking notes,
and trying to look professional. I straightened my clip-on tie and
checked my phone to see if Dad had called.

"The essence of news is death," Epistell said. "The rest is just
distraction. Someone once wrote, 'death is not an event in life:
we do not live to experience death.' But obituaries are events in
life. Only they connect us with the dead. My question to you is:
what can or should we say about the dead? For instance, what do
we think of this obituary?"

The screen displayed a smudged obituary with identifying
details removed. We contorted our necks to see: "[REDACTED],
48, of Chester, Pennsylvania expired Thursday evening in a house
fire. She was predeceased by her mother, [REDACTED], father,
[REDACTED], and one child, [REDACTED]. She is survived by
her husband, [REDACTED]. A wake will be held at Shankley's
Funeral Home on Saturday, December 15th, at 9 a.m."

Epistell was a gaunt man with a receding hairline and the
scars of burns around the area from his nose to his forehead,

rippling the sloughed flesh and cartilage above both ears. There was a sense of exhaustion and despair surrounding him, with his wrinkled clothes and tendency to look abstractly into the distance, muttering to himself and pinching the bridge of his nose when he removed his glasses. He reminded me of Dad.

For the past two weeks, we freelancers had attended meetings convened to address and promote the policies, standards, and values of the newspaper's staff and corporate sponsors. On multi-paged forms and photocopied documents, we'd provided our names in printed, signed, and initialed iterations; we received auto-generated PCU passwords, Lotus Notes™ identifications, Kronos® accounts, cafeteria cards, and assigned cubicles with the latest edition of the *Associated Press Stylebook and Briefing on Media Law* aligned on angled plastic trays. During lunch breaks the women sat over salads sharing pictures of children, while the older men smoked in hurried puffs behind the green garbage bins outside and I called Dad to see what he wanted me to pick up for dinner. He was too weak to cook now, and I—even though I was thirty-three—had never learned to prepare anything besides packaged pasta or baked potatoes.

Dad, the transportation director at Everett High School for thirty years, had recently been placed on medical leave by the school board in recognition of his prostate cancer, but most people in the district knew this provided a timeframe to allow an investigation into his decision not to cancel school during inclement weather on Monday, January 17th, when sophomore Megan Coakley's car swerved on black ice on Upper Valley Road and plunged through the frozen surface of Hesson Creek.

It was the first time in thirty years that he had not reported to work. He was increasingly frail, especially on days when he received chemo treatments at Temple's oncology unit, and when he sat on the couch to watch the Weather Channel or old family videos, still wearing the tweed suits and shined Oxfords he'd worn to work, it was as if he were sinking into the cushions. Sometimes he forgot my name and just called me "Son." On treatment days, he didn't even recognize me without his glasses. I no longer perceived my dad as a DAD, as if he were merely a category or archetype, but as a person, an idiosyncratic and imperfect and unique human being I had never known. It was only as I approached the age he had been when I was born, thirty-five, and was myself diagnosed with acid reflux disease and, more recently, hemorrhoids (which reminded me of Solar Anus, Megan Coakley's brother's band in high school), that I perceived how alike we were, as evidenced by the TUMS we consumed in daily handfuls or the container of hemorrhoidal wipes we shared in the bathroom with the good shitter.

When I watched him receiving his chemotherapy drip, I couldn't help but notice how vulnerable and scared he looked with his glasses removed. I wanted to know about Dad's pain and the pain of others, especially those like Epistell, who I could tell were on the verge of breaking apart fantastically, with sparks and the sounds of echoed drums, bringing others down with them in a spectacular tumult of concealed rage. I was afraid I might do the same.

Epistell orbited around the room, his meandering steps paralleling his meandering thoughts. "Perhaps we hope that obituary readers are tricked," he said, "that we can compose a false identity, a better identity for those we've loved. A plastic surgeon's death-mask, as it were. If we truly love the deceased, however, how can we lie? Why would we?" His thoughts sounded scripted, the questions rhetorical and speculative.

"Should we describe multiple lives, then?" he continued. "Is a true obituary an infinite description or an ethical gesture?" This final idea seemed to cause him great angst. Epistell looked out the window, as if the gray city, with its statues and roads and bridges named for the dead, were itself a larger memorial providing an answer to the questions that plagued him.

Nobody said anything.

I thought of my deceased older brother, John, strapped down on the hospital bed, machines going in and out of him, beeping and making exhaust sounds. I was ten then, curled under the bed listening to his cracking voice, screeching and metallic now like Grandma's, asking me not to tell Mom and Dad. He told me it wasn't an accident, begged me to unplug him from the machines, and I cried, silently, unnoticed by the nurses monitoring him.

Epistell returned to the lectern, flipping open the laptop and mousing around until a photograph of a blonde in a red 1970s swimsuit appeared beside the caption, "A Well-Acted Life."

"I had this poster on my bedroom wall," Epistell said, looking down with a kind of sad reverence. "She was called the most beautiful woman in the world then." He moved the mouse again and the image of an elderly woman in a wheelchair appeared. The woman looked like something formed out of melted Play-Doh.

"This is the same woman," Epistell said, "during the terminal stage of colon cancer. She was literally eaten from the inside, consumed by herself." He manipulated the screen so that the two images converged. "So, which is the actual person?" he asked. "How do we decide which image signifies the person? We think of the person how he or she looked when that person was most that person—but for us, right? Like she," he said, nodding toward the figure in the red bathing suit, "was the *Most Farrah Fawcett*, so to speak, of her entire life, in this picture. But who gets to decide? Why us? What makes our version more real than that of the boy she danced with in sixth grade who never forgot the feel of her hair's permed curls, or the Bangladeshi family she raised money for, or the Peruvian hospice worker holding her hand and praying to Jesus when she died?"

Epistell removed a pile of folders from a shelf inside the lectern and leafed through them, muttering names to himself: Smathey, Adams, Eaton, Chan, Morowitz, Coakley. He distributed these folders as we looked at the various eerie materials, comprised of data sheets, medical records, and scanned pictures. I received Megan Coakley. He returned again to the window, his burned face turned away from us, looking out over Philadelphia's naval yard and defunct sports complex, where workers placed pylons around memorial statues. The slush a different shade of black than the asphalt, the cars on the George C. Platt Memorial Bridge static, pluming exhaust fumes over the void. Everything was gray, the color of Dad's eyes.

"The project will be to compose real obituaries," Epistell said, turning back. "Obituaries that honor the singularity of the dead. We will be *describing lives*, not reducing them to clichés or lists of relatives and dates." He returned to the laptop and clicked back to the first slide, to the blotted-out obituary. "We will create actual holy testaments to the fact that a singular human being once existed. You have all received a person: Honor him or her. Narrate, illustrate, exposit, memorate, singulate. Describe a life."

୫୦ରେ

Dad and I chewed in silence. We used dishtowels as napkins. Dad changed the channel from the local news to the Weather Channel to the local news again. There had been no observable behavioral changes in Dad since the beginning of his medical leave. He still followed the same routine that he had since I was a teenager, rising at 4:30 to drink coffee and to study the weather patterns, and then visiting John's tombstone in the cemetery down the street. All of this he did in his slippers, and it was always 6:15 when he put on his professional shoes and I'd wake up to the sound of them clicking on the hardwood floor above my basement room as he opened the door to say, "Rise and Shine, Bucko!" Since the treatments started, his steps were shuffles, his voice breaking as he called down.

He got us two more lite beers and changed the TV's input setting, wobbling on his knees before the VCR, inserting a VHS, and rewinding to a Phillies game where John performed the National Anthem with the rest of the Everett High School Band. Our family had been seated in a special glass booth with old men who let me play with their rings. One of them owned the team before selling it to a group of investors who changed the stadium name from one that honored America's veterans to some kind of banking consortium. The stadium before Veteran Stadium had been named after Dad's favorite coach as a kid, Connie Mack. Dad always said that what he liked about Connie Mack was that he was who he was and said what he said. He hadn't been to the stadium since the name change, which seemed so stupid to me as a kid, like everything else he did then, stupid and inhuman.

I increasingly thought about how, when he was my age, he had a mortgage and a spouse and children, while it was a minor miracle if I could meet a girl online or keep a job for more than a month. The fact that my dad, whose expectations for me had once been so high, had finally stopped lecturing me and had seemingly accepted that my identity was that of a fat, balding, bachelor who lived in the basement surrounded by boxes of John's things, made the experience worse. I felt like I was who I was, finally, and that I was too old to change or improve. My emotions about this ranged from silent resignation to angry outbursts that would cost me jobs or friends, and also increased my blood-pressure according to my psychiatrist.

"Look, Dad," I said, pointing to the TV. There were helicopters and news vans surrounding two cars blasted together, an ambulance angled close, and EMTs with gurneys moving around.

"I suppose they'll blame me for that, too," he muttered.

We chewed again in silence, my dad with a napkin tucked into his collar, drinking his beer out of a wine glass, cutting his meatloaf into perfectly regular squares.

"There's something we should see, something that'll help."

I shrugged and continued chewing, removing a withered sliver of cardboard from my cheesesteak and sliding it under the cushions.

"Help who?" I asked.

⁝

We parked on the road above the Hesson Creek, looking down upon the void. Moonlight sheened off the snow and the ice on the guardrail and the train tracks above. Urine and ash left by tires, cigarettes, and the scattered embers of fires blemished the purity of the snow. The guardrail fractured into two rusted tendrils at Megan Coakley's crash site. Tracks from the Life Flight copter were still visible in the field, two depressions frozen into the hardened expanse of snow trampled where the memorants congregated. Flames flickered from a metal barrel by the Life Flight tracks.

A few feet away from group around the fire was an improvised memorial featuring a collection of people's offerings and Megan's belongings that we could see when we zoomed in with Mom's birdwatching binoculars: photos of Megan giving the finger to the camera, clothing sewn into swaying flags and banners, ripped and dirty stuffed animals, a poster of *The Scream* with her face photoshopped in, concert stubs, detention slips, disciplinary notices, police citations, her final yearbook photo with her head shaved and studs in her nose. They sat on the roofs of cars drinking and throwing cigarettes or flammable objects into the fire.

This was the second memorial.

Our high beams blanketed the field, like flashlights of the hovering dead.

"I called the police," Dad said. He leaned over the glove compartment with the binoculars.

The first memorial had been the day before. I remembered that everything in the Coakley house in Radley Run had been vacuumed, dusted, and polished, the magazines on the coffee table arranged in a fan-shape. Neighbors and relatives walked through the rooms expressing condolences and looking at pictures of Megan on the mantel, placing Hallmark cards in the kitchen next to the pasta salad. My dad stood there alone before that same yearbook picture of Megan Coakley that her parents had digitally modified to provide her with hair and to remove the studs, the photo enlarged and placed above the fireplace. Dad wore a navy-blue suit with short pants and white socks, a wool cap to cover his baldness. I remember thinking he looked like that mailman from *Cheers*, and how my embarrassment about him as a kid prevented me from inviting my friends over, when John was alive and Mom still lived with us.

"I mean that morning," my dad said quietly. "I was here when it happened, was about to call in a cancelation when..." He paused. "I heard the sound."

He hesitated. "I swear I was about to call. About to cancel."

I sort of patted his shoulder and said, "I believe you," thinking again of John's secrets and Megan Coakley's obituary.

That night I sat in the office parking lot in Dad's Buick Regal writing memories of John, everything he had asked me to hide, and left them in an envelope sticking out of the compartment between the driver and passenger seats. I entered the office at 3 a.m. I looked at pictures in various cubicles and inspected cabinets and pockets of jackets draped over the backs of chairs, noticing how some people cleared their stations like they would never leave and others left as if evacuated. The other team members' assignments were on their desks or, in some cases, aligned on the tray. More than half had begun composing obituaries according to the template push-pinned to their cubicles' cushioned panels; some wrote bullet points on legal pads or on their computers' word-processing software.

Cubicle six's subject was a fifty-year-old man from Lansdowne who'd suffered a myocardial infarction on SEPTA R3. There was a calendar of different beers from around the world turned to the wrong month on the contractor's corkboard. He had written, "Dennis Smathey loved the Phillies, the Eagles, and a medium-rare steak" and then crossed it out. Cubicle three's subject was a seventy-three-year-old woman from Chester who "loved to barbecue and attend to her eighteen grandchildren," as the freelancer had written. In the cubicle across from mine, there was a picture of an infant who had died at the age of two weeks. "Aubrey Starr Adams," the freelancer had typed, "passed peacefully from this world to fly with the angels. Although her life was short-lived, she showed a lifetime of love and laughter and will always be remembered as the happiest little munchkin on Earth." I sat at my desk and looked over what I had written about Megan Coakley earlier:

❧❧

Everyone agrees about Megan Coakley. Everyone who knew her, whether for years or even by short acquaintance, used the same words repeatedly. She was ambitious, confident, and successful in all her endeavors. She was respectful and hardworking. But most of all, she was adored. Megan Coakley—a fifteen-year-old Everett High sophomore and National Honors Society member, and winner of the "Leaders of the Future" essay contest—expired Monday morning after complications from an automobile accident.

❧❧

Then I noticed Epistell's office, located at the end of the row of cubicles between the breakroom and the darkened conference room. For some reason I felt attracted to it. There was a bamboo plant in one corner and moving boxes folded and stacked neatly, vertically aligned between a three-drawer cabinet and a bookshelf with annual hardback Pulitzers dating back to the 70s. The only thing on his desk beside his laptop was a picture of him and a woman wearing matching University of Maryland sweatshirts and pretending to attack a small child with lobster claws.

I opened Epistell's laptop and scrolled through the recently opened files. The camera in Epistell's office was mounted above the door, directed at his desk, I now know. I wasn't looking for anything in particular, as I told the security officials the next morning, but among the files I opened was the anonymous obituary that the team had seen earlier in the day, but without the details removed. Even with the details included, the obituary remained like those Epistell had been inveighing against. It wasn't a holy testament, but merely a list of facts, relations, and clichés.

I minimized the window and opened the one folder on the desktop, entitled "Lauren." It was dozens of pages long, with scattered anecdotes, the last modified date was around this time last night. I heard what sounded like one of the janitors down the hall, so I used my flash-drive to copy the file before slinking out of the office. Returning to my cubicle, I saw Epistell sitting in the shadows at the end of the aisle, holding crutches across his lap, as if expecting me.

"It's nice to have some company," he said.

I didn't know what to say. I held out my keys as if he would want them, which I realized made no sense.

"It's different here at night," he continued.

"Couldn't you have done for her what you want us to do for them?" I gestured toward Megan Coakley's file.

"I was in a coma for three weeks," he said, motioning to his crutches. "When I read it, I didn't even realize who it was about."

"So, this is all about your wife?" I asked. I felt myself wave my hands over the whole building, almost over the whole city, like everything for him had become about death and memory and how to reconcile the two, and somehow the whole city had become implicated.

He adjusted in his seat and crossed his long legs. "It matters for all of us," he said and shrugged. "I sometimes wonder how we can live our lives if we don't have a sense of our obituaries."

"One of my college professors made us write our own obituaries."

"You have practice then," he said.

"I didn't know what to write about myself, or what to imagine about my future. I pretended I was my brother and wrote his."

"It's ironic," he said.

"What is?"

"That the measure of a person's life is their obituary, but they have no control over how it's written."

We didn't talk about anything else then. He limped off somewhere into the grayer parts of the building. I turned on my monitor and closed the obituary I'd been writing about Megan Coakley. I inserted my flash-drive and opened the NIEMS Method file for Lauren Epistell, splitting the window with Megan Coakley's file. I tried to see Megan's (I remembered she liked to be called Meegan, at least as a little girl) life anew, quiveringly alive, to see it from within her, like some kind of existential flashlight that followed her everywhere, so that I was writing about her experience of the world, and not the world's experience of her. I compiled everything I could find—Insta and Tumblr, Google Image searches, newspaper articles, LexisNexis searches, blogs, Vimeo, to my own memories of her as a little girl playing with My Little Ponies when I bought pot from her brother. I sent Epistell an email with the subject line: "NIEMS Method" and attached the obituary, which now started with "Nobody agreed about Megan Coakley."

He commended me for it at the meeting convened at 9:30 a.m., saying even as a failure it was truer to the spirit of her unknown life than the fabricated attempts by the other team members, who had described not a life (with all of its contradictions) but rather a fictional stable identity. The meeting had been called by security, whose head ended it by terminating my employment me for stealing Epistell's (and by extension the corporation's) intellectual property. Epistell protested, mildly, nominally. He escorted me outside into the wind with his hand on my shoulder as he collected my office belongings—my IDs, my keys, my magnetized cards—as if I were setting off for a voyage, the voyage of death, like those people we had tried to resuscitate with words. And I imagined then all the survivors of the memorated dead, Mr. and Mrs. Coakley with their mantel of Hallmark cards, Dennis Smathey's widow rooting through shoeboxes for pension statements, Janice Adams on the floor beside the empty crib, nauseated from Effexor—and my dad, terminated from his life's one position but still impeccably dressed, parked out above the creek's void with John's obituary in his trembling hand—all of them reading Epistell's holy testaments in whatever gray light remained, all of them asking themselves, story after story after story, "Was that really you?"

Acknowledgements

For *THEM!*, my second family: (((Boomhauer))), Flounder, Freaky Fred, Skinny C, Schon, Hoss, Mikey S., Pais, H.D.— Perkins Diner, Citgo guy that sold us cigs, Q-Stix, The Laurels, VFW halls, *Punk Will Eat Itself*, mushroom truck accidents, 3rd-floor bathroom schwag & Saturday detentions. 1993—

I remember you all in my dreams

Allen Iverson, who saved my life during the 2000-2001 NBA playoffs

Howard Stern, who taught me to listen

Tawn Crowther, who taught me to drive manual

Mary Foltz, who taught me how to write, teach, and expansively love

Ann+Mike Nevin, & Uncle Paul: I treasure our Family Nights

Kurt Hoberg, my best reader

Emily Jane Rau, my Jersey Girl (*stick!*)

—My students: you are the still point of the turning world

—JTM, April 2020, St. Petersburg, FL

About the Author

James McAdams grew up in the suburbs of Philadelphia and currently resides in St. Petersburg, FL, where he teaches English at the University of South Florida, Ringling College of Art+Design, and Keep St. Pete Lit. He holds a Ph.D. in English from Lehigh University. His stories, poems, and essays have appeared in over fiftyy venues, including *Amazon/Day One, Bending Genres, Superstition Review,* and *B.O.A.T.T. Press.* He is Flash Fiction editor of *Barren Magazine* and is working on a novel-in-flash about the opioid epidemic. *Ambushing the Void* is his first book. *Ominem unius libri timeo.*

CPSIA information can be obtained
at www.ICGtesting.com
Printed in the USA
BVHW040524120620
581098BV00006B/114